Ski Mask Cartel 2

T.J. Edwards

Lock Down Publications and Ca$h Presents
Ski Mask Cartel 2
A Novel by *T.J. Edwards*

Lock Down Publications
P.O. Box 870494
Mesquite, Tx 75187

Visit our website
www.lockdownpublications.com

Copyright 2018 by T.J. Edwards Ski Mask Cartel 2

First Edition July 2018
Printed in the United States of America

This is a work of fiction. Names, characters, places, and incidents either are products of the author's imagination or are used fictitiously. Any similarity to actual events or locales or persons, living or dead, is entirely coincidental.

Lock Down Publications
Like our page on Facebook: Lock Down Publications
@
www.facebook.com/lockdownpublications.ldp
Cover design and layout by: **Dynasty Cover Me**
Book interior design by: **Shawn Walker**
Edited by: **Lauren Burton**

Stay Connected with Us!

Text **LOCKDOWN** to 22828 to stay up-to-date with new releases, sneak peaks, contests and more…

Submission Guideline.

Submit the first three chapters of your completed manuscript to ldpsubmissions@gmail.com, subject line: Your book's title. The manuscript must be in a .doc file and sent as an attachment. Document should be in Times New Roman, double spaced and in size 12 font. Also, provide your synopsis and full contact information. If sending multiple submissions, they must each be in a separate email.

Have a story but no way to send it electronically? You can still submit to LDP/Ca$h Presents. Send in the first three chapters, written or typed, of your completed manuscript to:

LDP: Submissions Dept
Po Box 870494
Mesquite, Tx 75187

DO NOT send original manuscript. Must be a duplicate.

Provide your synopsis and a cover letter containing your full contact information.

Thanks for considering LDP and Ca$h Presents.

Dedications

This book is dedicated to my amazingly, beautiful stomp down wife, Mrs. Jelissa Shante Edwards, who knows firsthand what this Ski Mask life is all about. I've had to feed our family many nights using that to make it happen. But, for you, I had to find another way because you deserve the best, and my place to be is beside you, protecting you at all times. You're my motivating force that keeps me going. No matter how old you get, you'll always be *my* baby girl. So, deal with it.

I love you forever and always.

Your husband.

Acknowledgments

Shout out to Cash and Shawn. I love ya'll with all my heart, not only as a C.E.O and C.O.O, but as brother and sister. This is me and my wife's home. You already know that our loyalty is sealed in blood. Mad love to the entire LDP family.

Much love and respect to my hittas: Von Walker, Antoine Drew Jr aka Burleigh Wood, Paul "Trey-Six" Westmoreland and my big homie Edward Wilson aka "E". Free ma dudes man and release these animals back to the jungles they were stripped from.

T.J. Edwards

Chapter 1

Wood jumped out of the car and slammed the door so hard it shook the vehicle. He frowned and upped a Mach .11, aiming it right at me while Vaughn took his cue and aimed his Mach .10 at Averie. I felt my heart thumping so hard in my chest I could barely breathe. They had caught me and Averie off guard.

"I knew we couldn't trust this bitch-ass nigga or that ho over there. Ain't no loyalty in you Chicago niggaz."

Before I could even reach for my gun, I saw the fire spit from his toolie, once again catching me off guard.

Boom, boom, boom!

I felt a bullet slam into my shoulder. It felt like somebody was shoving a big-ass broken piece of glass into it. I hollered and fell backward just as the second bullet hit me in the stomach and made me feel like I had swallowed a cup of acid. I hollered again, falling all the way to the ground as I felt my blood pouring out of me and onto the snow-covered ground.

"Damn, nigga. You actually killed dude's bitch-ass. What about this bitch right here?" Vaughn said, looking down at me.

I was in so much pain I wanted them to kill me. I had never felt anything like it before. I was about to holler out and call them niggaz a bunch of bitchez, so they'd finish me off when I heard the shots.

Boom! Boom! Boom!

Vaughn's head exploded and splattered all over my face before he fell on top of me. Wood looked around in a panic before the shots rang out again. This time I turned to my right and saw the fire spitting from the side of a garage about two yards down. *Boom! Boom! Boom! Boom!*

Two of the bullets slammed into Wood. knocking him backward. He fell to the ground and then crawled behind his car, bleeding from the chest and stomach. He looked over the car, stood up, and popped his Mach. *Boom, boom, boom, boom, boom!* The fire spit from the gun before he sat back behind the car, breathing hard.

The bleeding got worse, both his and mine. There I was, in the middle of the alley, bleeding out. The pain in my midsection was so bad I wanted to scream out loud. I looked down the alley and saw the masked gunman run from one garage to the next, getting closer to us. I didn't know who he was or where he'd come from, but I was hoping he would end my life and take me away from the pain. That shit was unbearable. I got to missing my daughter, Madison, and even Kenosha, her mother. I prayed they'd be okay after I was gone.

Wood stood back up on wobbly legs and shot over the car. *Boom, boom, boom, boom, boom, boom!* "Ah! You bitch-ass nigga! Show yo'self!" His gun's fire lit up the dark alley every time he pulled the trigger. The smell of gunpowder was heavy in the air, so much so I could taste it.

As Wood sat back down, he unloaded the clip hanging out of his Mach and reached for another when Averie came from the side of the garage holding a chrome .380. She ran right at him before he could get the new clip in.

Boom! Boom! Boom! Boom! Boom!

One bullet hit Wood after the next. His body slammed against the front of his car before he slouched over and started to shake. Averie stood over him and pulled the trigger again and again, causing the alley to light up. Then her gun started to click every time she pulled the trigger.

I felt like I was choking. I saw the earlier gunman running toward us, and I wanted to holler out to alert Averie, but it was too late. He made it all the way to her with his .40 Glock out, grabbed her by the throat, and held her up against the garage.

Then everything faded to black.

***

When I woke up, I was in a hospital bed with so many IV's in me I looked like a robot somebody was trying to put together. I felt hot and had sweat on my forehead. My vision was hazy. My shoulder and stomach hurt so bad it felt like I was being stabbed repeatedly. I opened my eyes wide and tried to sit up, but damn near passed back out from the pain.

Averie ran to my side and rubbed my chest, looking down on me with a concerned face. She looked like she wanted to cry. "Baby, you're going to be okay. You just gotta keep on fighting. Please keep on fighting, baby, because I need you," she cried. Her face became blurry, and I passed back out.

***

This time when I woke up, my cousin Tez was standing over me with an un-amused look on his face. He had his lips pushed all the way out and pulled tight in one corner. I opened my eyes to see him more clearly.

"Nigga, if you don't get yo' monkey-ass out this bed and jump back in these streets wit' me, I'm gon' kill yo' ass, fo' real. Get up, nigga!" he said so hard his dreads fell from over his shoulders and covered his chocolate face.

I blinked a few times, then tried to sit up. He rushed to help me. "Where am I, bro?" I asked, feeling sick on the stomach.

"Nigga, you in the hospital, and you been in this muthafucka for a few days. It's time you get yo' ass up out this bed and quit passing out 'n shit. Be thankful you alive, nigga. Get up!"

Averie rushed from the couch and moved him out of the way. "Damn, Tez, you ain't always gotta be so damn thuggish. He been shot a few times. Give him the room to recover." She frowned and looked down on me. "Baby, are you okay now? Is there anything I can do for you to make you feel better?" she asked, leaning down and kissing me on the cheek.

Averie had been Rayjon's woman before she crossed over to me. Before I got shot up, she and I hit that nigga for over a million dollars and ten bricks of heroin. I didn't know where none of that shit was now, but that was the first thing on my brain.

"Where is our shit at, Averie?" I asked with a voice so raspy it felt like I had sand in my throat.

"Y'all shit?" Tez moved Averie out of the way roughly. "Nigga, had I not come and popped them niggaz up, y'all asses would have been dead. So, I think it's best you call all that merch our shit." Tez cheesed and closed his eyes.

Averie pushed him back out of the way. "Damn, you just rude." She rolled her eyes at him. "Look, everything is safe and sound and put up. I didn't let Tez touch shit, but that nigga Rayjon looking for us. I mean he been fuckin' that city up since you went down. He in Jersey now, and I'm afraid who he finna bring back wit' him. I think we need to bounce or get our shit together, because it's finna be a war." She looked afraid.

Tez sucked his teeth. "Jo, I ain't worried 'bout that nigga because he trying to wage a war in our city like that shit sweet. Nigga, we 'bout whatever the fuck he 'bout. I got some grimy-ass project kids that's 'bout that action. We got enough paper to start our own cartel and to feed the hungry savages that's gon' be down wit' us. While you been in this hospital, I been on bitness. I can't wait to show you. It's going down," he said, overly excited.

Averie came to my other side and lay her cheek against mine. "Baby, I missed you. I don't know what we're going to do, but by the time you get out of this bed, I pray you have it all figured out."

After she said that, a black, heavy-set nurse came into the room with a gray afro. She walked up to me and put her hand on my forehead. "Well, look who's awake. That's good to see. How are you feeling, my darling?" She checked the machines and started to write on her clipboard.

I was feeling a stabbing pain in my stomach and shoulder, but before I had passed out the last time it felt ten times worse. "I feel okay, aside from the constant stabbing pain in my stomach and shoulder."

She smiled warmly. "Yeah, that's because we removed a bullet from both locations. But you should be thankful that there was no real internal damage. There will be some scarring, but other than that you should make a full recovery. You're a healthy young man. Thank God for that." She finished writing on her clipboard and sighed out loud. "Well, I guess you're just about ready to get out of here. I'll recommend you be released in forty-eight hours. How does that sound?" she asked, smiling.

Tez scrunched his face. "Too long, that's how that sound. Aye, me and the homie got bitness to take care of. He can't be sitting in here for no two mo' days. That's bullshit." He looked heated.

The nurse looked him up and down and raised her eyebrow. "Young man, maybe you should watch yo' mouth and be thankful your friend here is even alive, because in just the last eight hours there have been four men brought into this hospital with the same injuries he sustained, but they are now deceased. So, thank Jehovah for keeping him here and exercise more patience."

"Yeah, dang, Tez. I know you a gangsta and all, but sometimes you gotta hold that down and show some respect to your elders," Averie said before turning to the nurse. "Hey, ma'am, I'm sorry about that. We appreciate all you have done. If you feel like he needs another few days, then that's just that. You haven't failed us yet."

The nurse walked over and gave Averie a hug, then looked her up and down. "I bet you a nice, Christian girl, huh?"

Averie smiled, then nodded her head. "I believe, but I haven't been to church in a while. Soon, though."

The nurse smiled warmly. "It's okay, baby. I been slacking, too. You just keep an eye on these two and make sure you keep them in line. That's all I can ask for. And this one right here," she said, pointing over her shoulder with her thumb at Tez, "whenever you do decide to go back to church, you make sure you take him wit' you."

Tez curled his upper lip. "Muthafucka, I ain't even gon' have my funeral in a church. Fuck I look like? I don't get down wit' that fake shit. Ain't you got somethin' better to do than be all up in here preaching that nonsense? A muthafucka could be dying in the other room or somethin'. Why don't you make yo' rounds?" He mugged the shit out of her.

I sat up in the bed, feeling the sharp pains in my stomach. "Chill, nigga. All that ain't necessary."

The nurse shook her head and walked out of the room, mumbling to herself. I could tell she wanted to go off on him, and he had hurt her feelings. I thought that shit was bogus as hell, and I wanted to tear into Tez's ass, but I decided against it since I barely had any strength in me at that time.

But that didn't stop Averie from speaking her mind the minute the sista closed the door. She put her hand on her hip and looked at him for a few seconds. "Really, Tez? You think it's cool to treat that older woman like that? That *black* woman?" She said the word *black* strongly to emphasize her point.

Tez waved her off. "Look, I ain't got no time to be having respect for bitchez I don't even know. Fuck that lady. Once we leave this muthafucka, we ain't never gon' see her again. Damn. I ain't wit' all this soft shit."

Averie shook her head. "Look, that lady could have had Racine's ass in jail right now. Don't you know it's standard procedure for them to contact the authorities immediately when a person comes in wit' gunshot wounds? You know they was called when Racine was brought in. The only reason he wasn't in lock-up from the get-go was cuz he was in a coma. That lady was supposed to call the cops the moment he showed signs of waking up. It could have been detectives all over this place. Then what? Y'all been doing all kinds of shit all over Chicago. Only God knows if one of you is on their radar."

Tez waved her off. "I don't give a fuck what you talking about. If that bitch would have called the police on my cousin, I would have knocked her mutha-fucking head off with no mercy. I ain't playin' about my blood no more. We about to take over this city, and to be able to do that we can't be giving a fuck about people's feelings and shit. That goes for you hoez and all. That's on my momma. We gotta get up out this bitch before we get hit wit' a hard line of questionin'."

Averie bucked her eyes and looked like she wanted to snap out but held her tongue. I winced in pain. Had I not been feeling so weak, I would have gotten up and got on Tez's ass for the disrespect toward her. "Tez, it's good, cuz. You ain't gotta come at her like that. We all in this shit together. She done made sure we got all this money, so she gon' have to be the first lady of this cartel, and with that title comes the utmost respect."

I sat up further and felt like I wanted to throw up. The room seemed like it was spinning, and I had to take a few deep breaths just to calm myself.

Tez lowered his head. "Damn, yo. That's my bad, Averie, but y'all gon' have to miss me wit' all this soft shit, cuz. I ain't got that shit in me, so y'all can't expect for me to be nobody but me."

Averie looked at the ceiling and took a deep breath. "I am really curious to see how all of this is going to work out. Me personally, I am bowing down to you, Racine, as head of this body. And if that means I must bow down to Tez as well, then I will. All I ask for is a little respect. He gotta honor my woman-ness and my gangsta. Just like you'll bust that gun, Tez, so will I. You gon' put in work for this cartel, and I am too. I'll respect you, and I demand the same. You feel me."

Tez looked down at the floor the whole time she was talking, clenching his jaw off and on. It took him almost a full minute to reply to her. He nodded his head hard. "You know what? I can do that. I can respect your slot, but y'all can't expect for me to be like that wit' no other bitchez. I'm a man, and that ain't how life supposed to work. That nigga Racine just different or somethin'." He walked over to Averie and opened his arms.

She pursed her lips and gave him a look that said *mm-hm* before walking into his arms and hugging him. "Just do yo' best, Tez, and don't be trying to change Racine. He got his own swagger, and it works."

I heard what they were saying, but I was already fading in and out of consciousness. I took the nurse's advice and rested up for two more days before they released me back into the world after prescribing me Percocet-30s.

Chapter 2

I walked into the Super Eight Motel room Averie had booked right on the side of Interstate-94. It was a real seedy motel I would have never slept in even if a muthafucka paid me to. As soon as I walked in the door, a big-ass rat ran past my feet and out into the hallway. I jumped so high my head damn near touched the ceiling. The pain in my stomach wasn't as bad as long as I took the pills they gave me, but after being caught off guard by that rodent, the sudden movement reminded me of that injury all over again. I had to brace myself against the wall outside of the door.

Averie came and put her arm around me. "Baby, are you okay?"

I took a deep breath and blew it out real slowly before nodding my head. "Yeah, I'm a'ight. Let's just get in here so we can sit down for a minute." I wrapped my arm around her shoulder and leaned on her as we made our way into the room.

There were so many roaches all over the floor I was wonderin' how the motel was still in business. The room smelled like funk, and I could hear real loud moaning from the people next door because the walls were so thin. After I stepped in, Averie closed the door behind me and locked it. I took my time getting to the bed before sitting down on it, praying I didn't catch nothing from the blanket covering the bed.

Averie walked into the bathroom, then came back out with a duffel bag on her shoulder. She sat it on the bed, went back into the bathroom, and brought another one out, setting it next to the first one. She went a third time, returned with another duffle, and sat it beside the other two. "That's $1.5 million right there, and ten kilos of heroin. We can get $100,000 apiece for each one. If we sell them in weight, we can get forty apiece, easily." She unzipped all the bags and took a step back. "Since you been gon', I ain't touched one penny of this money because I honor you as the head of our body. From here on out, I'll never make a move unless it's beneficial to you first, and then myself. I'm riding for you through it all. All I ask is I am labeled the first lady of this cartel, and when you get big you don't switch the game up on me. I ain't trying to be yo' main bitch or nothin' because I know you got a baby momma, but I do need to possess a part of you."

She came in front of me and knelt down, looking up into my face. I looked down on her and nodded. "You got my word, and my loyalty for as long as we eating together. I honor you for the moves you made to get us this paper. Now just sit back and watch how I flip this shit." I pulled her up, then stood up myself, wrapped my arms around the small of her back and kissed her juicy lips for damn near two minutes.

When we finally stopped kissing, I noticed her nipples were hard as hell and threatening to bust through her white Fendi top. My dick was hard, too. I reached out and squeezed her breasts, one in each hand. They were firm and soft at the same time.

She moaned, stepped forward, and kissed me on the neck, before reaching between us and grabbing my dick. "Baby, you think you ready for me to sit on this dick? Huh? Because I need some of this so bad right now," she whimpered, then bit into my neck so hard I felt that animal growling deep within me.

I didn't know if I was ready to perform at my highest level with my stomach feeling like it was feeling, but I was damn ready to try. Averie had some bomb-ass pussy, and I couldn't wait to get back between them thighs. She was even the type of freak who liked for me to hit that ass, and that was a plus in my book. A female who would let a nigga use every hole on her body wit' no inhibitions drove me crazy. It was hard for me to turn them types down.

To answer her question, I reached behind her and gripped that big-ass booty encased in stretchy Fendi pants. That muthafucka was soft and round. I cuffed it and opened it a li'l bit. Averie had one of them booties that made a nigga do a double-take, even if he was wit' his bitch. She was small up top, kinda short, but once you got below her waist, she was thick as a mule and her pussy was always wet.

She moaned into my neck, bit it again, and worked my pants down to my ankles before helping me take them all the way off. Then came my boxers. At the same time, she pulled them down and off, she pulled her top over her head and unlatched her bra from the front, causing her brown titties to spill out. Both big nipples were already erect and fully engorged. She sat on the bed and lay on her back, pulling her pants down her thick thighs and off.

I noticed she had on a G-string that was stuck all up inside of her sex lips. As soon as I saw that shit, I crouched down and pulled her li'l thick ass to the edge of the bed, opened them thighs, and slurped her pussy into my mouth loudly. It was already wet and tasted salty.

"Uh! Fuck!" she moaned. "Here you go, already! Here you fuckin' go, Racine!" She opened her legs wider and tilted her head back with her mouth wide open.

I got to sucking and licking with little force, opening her sex lips so I could see that clit pop out, then I trapped it wit' my lips and sucked hard before sliding two fingers up her wet hole and running them in and out of her at full speed while I sucked harder and harder on her clit, constantly pulling the lips back wit' my other fingers. I was slurping so loud it was turning me on.

Averie got to humping into my face wit' her eyes closed. I could feel her body shaking, then she was humping into me harder.

"Uh! Uh! Shit! Racine! Racine! I! Can't! Take! This! Shit! Uh! My! Gawd!" She started shaking so hard my mouth slipped away from her clit, but I held onto them thick-ass thighs and trapped it again, feeling her squirt on my tongue.

After her shaking stopped, she got up and dropped down to her knees, took my dick, and kissed the head. "Am I still yo' bitch, Racine? Huh? Tell me who I am to you, daddy," she said before sucking my head into her mouth and spearing her head into my lap, sucking me so hard my toes were curling up. The warmth, the wetness, the tightness was doing somethin' to me. I grabbed a handful of her hair and humped into her face a little faster. "Yeah, baby. Yeah. Mm, shit. Yeah, you my–you my bitch. You my bitch now. Just suck this dick fo' daddy."

At hearing that, she got to sucking me so hard and fast I felt my nut building up in my balls. The loud noises she made wit' her mouth and the way she moaned around my dick was all too much. I gripped her hair harder and pumped into her mouth five more quick times, then released my seed. "Uh! Shit!"

Glob after glob exited me, and she kept on sucking loudly, moaning at the top of her lungs. She kept on sucking for so long that I stayed hard.

She got up and bent over the bed, spreading her legs, and pulling her thick ass cheeks apart, the scent of her pussy already in the air. "Fuck this pussy now, Racine. I need you to fuck me as hard as you can, baby. Please. I just need yo' dick inside of my body," she whimpered, biting into her bottom lip. She reached under herself and started playin' wit' her clitoris, pinching it and rubbing it hard.

I stepped up behind her, stroking my dick, then ran my dick head up and down her crease, coating it with her juices before pushin' it into her hot pocket.

"Mm, yes, daddy. I'm yo' bitch. Now fuck this pussy. Fuck yo' bitch, daddy." She slammed her ass back into my lap, forcing my dick all the way into her middle.

I put the pain in my stomach to the side and let all my feeling concentrate on the ecstasy her pussy was giving me. I grabbed her hips and got to wearing that ass out. *Bam. Bam. Bam. Bam. Bam. Bam. Bam.*

"Ah, fuck. Fuck me, daddy. Fuck me!" she screamed, and I could feel her walls sucking at me hungrily.

I grabbed a handful of her hair again, causing her to arch her back, and really got to hitting that pussy.

Every time I crashed into her ass, it jiggled along wit' her thighs. That shit motivated me to go harder and harder until she came, then caused me to cum minutes after.

After we got done doing the do, we showered, and I had to switch up my bandages. She helped me do that before we went back into the bedroom area. I got to missing my daughter, Madison.

"Yo, Averie, what you think that nigga Rayjon finna be on? You think he 'bout to bring some real heat our way when he gets back in town?" I just wanted to know what she was seeing. After all, she had been wit' the nigga for a long time, so she had to know his habits and what he was capable of.

She sat on the bed and pulled her panties up her thick thighs before standing up and pulling them all the way up. I liked the way the string separated her ass cheeks. Her li'l thick-ass had a body that kept me aroused just from looking at it. After she put her panties back on, she stepped into her Fendi pants and reached for her top, which was on the small nightstand next to the lamp. "I think he finna raise hell. I already know when he catches me he gon' kill me, which is why we gotta get our shit in order so when he do bomb, we'll be able to bomb back on his ass. I know he can't do nothin' major right now because he ain't got no money. I took it all, so he probably went back to Jersey to hit a bunch of licks. Once he gets his paper up, he gon' be back on bitness. I know that for a fact. He ain't finna take this shit lying down. That nigga come from a family of savages."

I personally didn't give a fuck where that nigga came from. I already knew me and Tez were about to build a cold-hearted army of monsters. I already told my cousin a long time ago that whenever I built up a mob, I didn't want nothin' in it but young, hungry, outta-they-minds, project li'l niggas who didn't give a fuck about shit but money and loyalty. I already knew where to cop my li'l killas from, and I couldn't wait to get shit started, although Tez already said he had.

I put my hand on my stomach. "Well, I'ma tell you like this, it's about to be a muthafuckin' war, because ain't shit sweet. By the time that nigga get his weight up, we gon' have our shit in order, mark my words."

I told Averie I needed to get up wit' my baby mother, Kenosha, and see my daughter, Madison, and she agreed. I had the nigga Tez come and scoop me up, and from the minute I sat in the truck all he could talk about was me meeting some of the li'l killas he had chosen to be down wit' our cartel.

"Jo, I'm telling you, when you meet these li'l savages, you gon' already get the vibe we finna be hurting shit. I made sure the niggaz I chose was gon' be about that life. These niggaz so hungry I found 'em eating out of a garbage can, cuz."

I shook my head because I couldn't believe no shit like that. I felt like Tez was jacking and trying to oversell the li'l niggaz. "Cuz, I ain't believing no shit like that. You doing too much," I laughed.

He frowned. "I ain't lying, nigga. On my momma. I'm talking straight eating out of that garbage can in the back of White Castle over on 63rd. You know they usually lock them dumpsters up, but these li'l niggaz broke the locks, and all three of them were getting it how they live. Starving, nigga."

I wanted to meet them after hearing that. That sounded real bad to me. I wondered what had happened to them that had them doing some shit like that. "Well, I can't wait to see what yo' recruiting look like, because the li'l niggaz I get gotta be from the projects. That's the criteria."

When I opened the door to my crib, my daughter was sitting on the couch, playin' on her tablet, I guess. When she saw me, she screamed so loud I heard a dish in the kitchen drop and break.

"Daddy!" she hollered and ran across the front room to jump into my arms. I caught her and felt a li'l pain in my stomach that caused me to exhale loudly, but I shook it off. She wrapped her little arms around my neck as Kenosha came out of the kitchen with a look of surprise written across her face.

I kissed my baby girl. "I missed you, li'l momma. I was thinking about you the whole time I was gone. Do you hear me, baby?"

She nodded her head and put her face into the crook of my neck. "I was scared when you were gone, Daddy. I thought you wasn't coming back because you were mad at me," she whimpered, and then started to cry.

I moved her back from my chest and kissed her soft cheek. "Baby, I can never get mad at you. You're my baby girl, and I love you with all of me. You're my little angel, do you hear me? I will never leave you."

She nodded her head, then put her face back into the crook of my neck. I could still hear her sniveling.

Kenosha looked angry. She walked right up to me and stood in my face. "Madison, go play in yo' room now!" She pointed down the hall.

Madison raised her face from my neck. "But I miss my daddy, and I just wanna –"

Kenosha cut her off. "Madison, if you don't get yo' ass down and go do like I say, I'm gon' whoop yo' ass in front of yo' daddy. Now go!" she hollered, and I could tell she was getting ready to snap.

I lowered Madison to the carpet. "Baby, just do what she say. That way you don't get in trouble. I'll be in your room later to spend some time wit' you." I kissed her on the cheek and patted her on the butt. "Go, li'l ma."

She lowered her head and slowly walked down the hallway toward her room. Seeing her body language made me feel bad as hell. I know my daughter missed me, and her mother ain't have no right for snapping on her like that. I was gon' check Kenosha, but I wasn't gon' do it in front of our daughter.

"So, where the fuck you been at? Because Tez wouldn't tell me shit," she asked, stepping into my face.

I took a step back and held my hands out to create some space because I didn't like when nobody got in my face. It made me feel on edge, and on top of that, my temper was horrible. I had never put my hands on Kenosha before, but I'd gotten close 'cuz she had a habit of jumping in my face every time she felt some type of way. "Kenosha, step yo' ass back."

She stepped forward again and moved my hands out of the way. "Nall, fuck that. I wanna know what bitch you fucking wit' that done had you out for damn near a month straight. You ain't called nobody or told nobody shit. Nigga, you bogus."

Tez stood by the front door with his head tilted back, looking at the ceiling like he couldn't believe I was letting her come at me like that. I could see his nostrils flaring.

I raised my shirt and showed her my bandages. "I got popped twice, and I ain't want you and Madison to see me all fucked up. A couple niggaz caught me slipping before Tez stepped in and handled that bitness."

Kenosha's eyes got big, then she blinked back tears, putting her hand lightly on my bandage. "Oh my God, baby, I'm so sorry. I didn't know," she cried. "I could have lost you." She shook her head. "I swear to God, if I would have lost you, I would have taken my own life. I love you so much, Racine."

I wrapped her into my arms while Tez rolled his eyes and shook his head. "I'm good, though. I'm almost fully recovered, so don't sweat it."

Even though me and Kenosha had a daughter together, we weren't technically a couple. I mean, I loved her and everything, and I would do anything for her, but we weren't hollering that one-on-one shit. I let her do her, and she let me do me. I felt like we were too young for anything else.

She broke into a fit of tears while I held her and walked her to my bedroom, sitting on the bed wit' her. She put both of her hands over her face, shaking her head. "Racine, every time you leave out of that door, I be scared for yo' life because I know how you and Tez get down. I swear, I don't know what I would do if somethin' more serious happened to you.

You're my whole entire life outside of Madison. I know I wouldn't be able to take that.

I didn't like when she talked like that. I didn't see myself leaving the planet no time soon, but if that was to happen, then I was gon' make sure her and my daughter was well taken care of and never needed for nothin'. That was my number one objective. "Baby, stop worrying about that kind of shit. I got this. I gotta make shit happen for you and our baby, and from time to time I gotta eat slugz. That's just the way the game goes, and I'm taking it in stride. You just know that, before it's all said and done, we gon' be filthy rich and covered in dirty money. Now mark those words."

Chapter 3

Four days later I wasn't feeling no pain in my gut, and I felt ready to step out into the slums. I jumped in my truck just as it began to snow and met up wit' Tez at the Robert Taylor Home Projects. When I pulled up, he was standing in front of the building wit' two niggas, and they were gathered around a burning metal garbage can like they were bums trying to stay warm. He must've saw my truck, because he slowly made his way over to me in a leather Gucci jacket with a black fur Gucci hat on his head. I rolled down my window.

"Nigga, you showed up at the right time. I'm 'bout to show you how these li'l niggaz get down. Then I'm gon' tell you why I called you to this project. Let's go."

That nigga Tez was always on something, so I figured he had something up his sleeve. I jumped out of my Navigator and zipped up my Marc Jacobs leather, adjusting the matching fur hat on my head. The wind was blowing hard as hell, and it was already below zero outside. I made sure my Glock .40 was secure on my waist and my vest was as tight to my chest as possible.

When I got in front of the door to the project, one of the niggaz Tez was standing wit' looked me up and down wit' a mug on his face. He was real skinny and looked grimy. "What's good, nigga?"

I curled my upper lip. "Fuck you mean, *what's good nigga*? What's good wit' you?" I asked, stepping into his face with a mug just as evil as his. I ain't know who this li'l nigga thought he was, but I had visions of bodying his ass right there.

Tez laughed. "Yo, you niggaz chill." He stepped in between us and separated us. "Racine, this my li'l killa, Wayne. Wayne, this my cousin, nigga. And if you ever come at him bogus like that again, I'll leave you in front of these buildings stanking. Do you feel me?"

Wayne's mug softened just a li'l bit. "Yeah, I feel you, chief. That's my bad. I ain't know who he was. You already know how I get down."

I mugged the fuck out of li'l dude. "Yeah, nigga, and he know how I get down, too. So, take his advice." I brushed past him and stood in front of the other nigga, who was yellow and heavyset. "And who might you be, li'l homie?"

He pulled his black skullcap down over his ears and blew into his left hand. "My name E. This my nigga, right here, and we ready to blast for this cartel, we ready to show you how we get down."

The wind picked up speed, and I felt like my face was freezing over. "A'ight then, I guess I'm finna see. So, what's good?" I asked, looking at Tez.

We made our way up twelve flights of stairs. The stairwells smelled like piss and shit. On a few of the landings there were dope fien's four or five deep smoking the pipe, and on other landings there were some shooting heroin into their veins. We got to one landing and there was a naked woman lying dead right on the stairs. She had a cord wrapped around her right arm, and the syringe she'd used to shoot up her dope was still left in her arm. Her eyes were wide open, and her body was starting to swell up and decompose. She smelled like boiled tampons. We all stepped over her, but I leaned down and closed her eyes. I felt that was the best I could offer her in that moment.

"That's why we gotta take over shit around here, because it's been plenty dope heads dying off this dope these niggaz been servin'. And they ain't dying because it's good dope, they dying because it's bull-shit," E said, shaking his head.

"Don't even worry about that, li'l homie. This building on the list of priorities, you best believe that."

We kept on taking the stairs until we got to the twelfth floor. Once there, we were met by four dudes with blue rags around their necks and black skull-caps.

Wayne walked up to one of them and shook his hand in a gang manner. "What up, BD?"

"Shit, we finna go make some money the ski mask way. You already know what it do," the fat nigga said.

Wayne nodded. "Already know. What you should be is trying to get down wit' my niggaz right here, 'cause they finna take over the Taylors. This muthafucka in need of new management, and you're seeing them right now in living color." Wayne took a step back and smiled.

I noticed all four of the niggaz we were looking at frowned. The fat nigga was the first to look me up and down before shaking his head. "Nall, Jo. BD run this muthafucka right here. I don't know who homie and them is, but ain't shit moving. Trust me on that."

E stepped in front of me and Tez wit' his hand under his shirt. "Well, I don't give a fuck what you niggaz talking about. Y'all got y'all first warning right now. When the takeover come, it's gon' be too late." He scrunched the right side of his face, and his eyes got low.

The fat nigga took a step back and bumped into his crew, who were looking on with their eyes wide. "Yo, Wayne, yo' cousin always on that dumb shit. Tell homie to calm down. Shit ain't that serious." He looked a little worried.

Wayne curled his upper lip. "Oh, but it is. You niggaz gon' see in time, though. I'll holla." He shook up wit' the fat nigga again and we made our way down the hallway.

Tez wrapped his arm around E. "Nigga, that's why I fuck wit' you, li'l dawg. I'm gon' make sure you get that slot you deserve in this cartel. That's my word."

E nodded his head and continued to follow behind Wayne. I liked how he'd just got down, and I couldn't wait to fuck wit' that li'l nigga out in the field.

The hallway smelled like piss and had all kinds of graffiti on the walls, mainly repping BD's street gang. There were drawings of the roman numeral three and the Star of David, though every one of those stars I seen had a zig-zag going down the middle of it, meaning the BD's were saying fuck the gang it represented.

When we got to the end of the hallway, we stopped in front of a door that said Twelve D. Wayne took some keys out of his pocket and placed one into the lock before pushing the door in.

Tez slapped his hand on my shoulder. "Nigga, wait until you see this shit." He laughed and walked in behind Wayne, and I followed him.

The first thing I noted when I stepped into the place was it didn't have any furniture and there was trash all over the floor, mixed with at least a thousand big-ass cockroaches. They crawled all over the apartment. On top of that, there were rats running along the wall and feasted on a big pile of garbage in the kitchen. It smelled like something was spoiled somewhere in the apartment, and it was cold as hell in there. I could tell there wasn't any heat on.

E stepped in front of the hallway that led to the back of the apartment. "Come on, y'all. I'm 'bout to show Racine how me and my cousin get down for that paper."

He started to walk down the hallway with us behind him. Smack dab in the middle of it was a dead cat with its mouth wide open. Five big rats were eating away at its midsection. Blood leaked out of its body and pooled around the animal while roaches crawled all around. As we walked past, the rats didn't run or stop gnawing away at its flesh or anything. That shit blew my mind. I felt itchy as hell.

We got to a bedroom door and E opened it. I looked inside, and before I could see anything, I heard a bunch of murmuring. Then, as I stepped in behind him, I saw three people lying on the floor, duct-taped with roaches crawling all over them. I frowned. "Who the fuck is these niggaz?" I asked Tez.

He smiled, unzipped his leather jacket, and scratched under his vest. "These the niggaz that sell that weak-ass dope out this building. They the homie E's uncles, and after we told them it was finna be new management and they gotta move around, they had a whole lot to say. So, we finna watch our li'l niggaz prove they loyalty to us right now."

E shrugged his shoulders and pulled a box cutter from his left front pocket. "You ain't saying shit, big homie. Far as I'm concerned, fuck these niggaz. They ain't never did shit for me or my moms other than feed her drug habit. I'ma take pleasure in murking they ass, especially my bitch-ass oldest uncle, right here."

He pulled one of the bound yellow niggaz by the leg until he was directly under him, then sat on his chest and pulled the duct tape from his mouth. "Bitch-nigga, what's yo' last words before I take you out the game? And don't get to begging fo' yo' life, 'cuz that shit over wit'." E said through clenched teeth.

The yellow nigga swallowed. "Nephew, you ain't gotta do this shit. We'll move around, my nigga. We'll go out west and fuck wit' BD an' 'em out there. That's my word, man. Y'all can have this building."

E grabbed his throat and forced the back of his head to the stained carpet. "Yo, I pledge my loyalty to you, Tez, and to you, Racine. Blood in and blood out, my nigga." He whipped the box cutter through the air and sliced his uncle across the face repeatedly while the man hollered and tried to wiggle against him with no success. Blood got to popping into the air as gash after gash opened on his face, yet E kept on going. "Bitch. Nigga. Ain't. Never. Did. Shit. Fo'. Me. Or. My. Momma!" he hollered, slicing the man's face up so bad I could see his bone and the muscles underneath his skin.

All the while the man continued to holler and scream until all at once he stopped. E stood up with a big puddle of blood under his Eastland boots. He wiped his mouth with the back of his hand, blood dripped from his box cutter. "Fuck that nigga, Jo. Bitch-ass nigga started my moms off on that shit. I couldn't wait to kill him one day."

Wayne shrugged his shoulders. "Damn. Oh well. I ain't got no box cutter, but I do got this muthafucka right here." He picked up a hammer leaning against the wall I hadn't paid attention to. He sat on the next duct-taped man's chest and smiled down at him. "Look, I ain't got shit to say to you, homie. It's lights out." He looked up at Tez, and then me. "I pledge my loyalty to you niggaz, blood in and blood out." He raised the arm with the hammer in it before bringing it down so fast and hard the front of it got stuck in the man's skull.

As soon as it was implanted, the duct-taped dude started to holler into his tape while he shook on the carpet like he was having a seizure, and he probably was. Wayne jiggled the hammer until it popped out of his skull, leaving a massive hole. Blood poured out like tomato soup and ran down the right side of the man's face while he continued to shake.

Tez clapped his hands together. "Yo, these my li'l niggaz. Fuckin' animals. Kill that nigga, Wayne.

Finish his bitch-ass!" he hollered, throwing his arm around my shoulders.

I could smell the blood of the two niggaz, and it was making me feel sick. That shit was strong, like they were unhealthy or something. Blood is just like piss, somewhat. Just like how piss stinks worst when someone ain't been drinking the right amount of water, it's the same way wit' blood. Often when I killed a nigga, I could tell by the smell of their blood whether they took care of themselves or not, and these niggaz smelled like they didn't.

Wayne raised the hammer again and brought it down, smashing it into the dude's face, so he stopped moving altogether. Wayne slammed the hammer into his forehead one last time, even though it was pointless, and stood up with the hammer still in his hand, saturated wit' blood. He looked down on the man wit' his chest heaving up and down.

I pointed at the other dude. "What about him?" He was lying on his side, curled into a ball. I could tell he was scared out of his mind by the way he was shaking.

Tez walked over to him and bent down. "He is what you call our TMZ. This nigga gon' be the one to let the hood know how we get down. After what he just saw, you better believe he gon' get the word out." He snatched the duct tape from the li'l niggaz's mouth. "Nigga, you see how we get down?"

He shook his head, slobber running out of his mouth and on down his cheek. "Yeah, man. I swear I don't want no problems. Please don't kill me. I'll tell whoever what y'all want me to. Just don't kill me like them."

He sounded all whiney and shit, and it was getting me irritated. I hated when tough niggaz acted like bitchez when it was time to meet that reaper.

E walked over and kicked him in the stomach so hard he slid a little bit backward. "Shut yo' soft-ass up, nigga. If we was gon' kill you, we'da did that already."

I ain't know what was on that nigga Tez's mind, but I wasn't on leaving no witnesses. I knew that would be dumb as hell. "Bruh, what the fuck we need this nigga's word of mouth fo'? If muthafuckas ain't trying to honor what we on, then we make' 'em feel this steel, point-blank. I ain't wit' this 'leaving this nigga alive' shit. Fuck that." I pulled out my pistol and stood over the dude's ass.

Tez jumped up and got out of the way. "Fuck him, then. If you ain't on that, then neither am I." He pulled his pistol out and aimed it at the last dude along wit' me.

"Please, don't kill me, man. Please. I'll do anything. I'm beggin' y'all, bruh. I'll do —"

E dropped down to his knees in front of the nigga, took his pistol, and slammed it down his throat so far, he started to gag over the barrel. "I hate crybabies, Jo." *Boom! Boom!* The back of the dude's head exploded and splattered against the carpet. E stood up and looked down on him. "Let's hit some licks now, bruh. I gotta put some clothes on my son's back."

Chapter 4

Kenosha had been walking around the house in silence for two days straight, and I could tell something was wrong wit' her, but she wasn't saying shit. So, two days after we bodied them niggaz over in the Robert Taylors, I thought it was best I took her out to dinner. That way we could talk, plus it had been a minute since I had done anything like that for her, and I felt it was time. So that morning I woke her up with a CoCo Chanel dress and some red-bottom heels, some yellow diamond earrings, and a matching yellow diamond tennis bracelet and told her I wanted to spend the night out wit' her and we could go eat anywhere she wanted to. The night was hers.

She picked a nice li'l cozy spot called Rashad's on 149th out in Harvey, Illinois, which is another suburb out of Chicago. The place is where most of the upper crust hip-hop successes went to lean back and just enjoy a good meal. The restaurant was dimly-lit and had an older woman on the stage singing a soft Sade number. The feeling was smooth, and I felt at peace for the moment. My stomach wasn't bothering me. Neither was my shoulder. And even though I had large sums of money on my mind, I felt like it was important I knew what was going on wit' my BM.

I looked across the table and into her pretty face and smiled. She lowered her head and took a deep breath before exhaling. I reached across our table and laid my hand on top of hers. "Baby, what's the matter? Why do you seem so down to me?" I asked, really concerned. My BM meant the world to me.

She shrugged her shoulders. "I don't know, baby. I guess I'm still trying to get over the fact you could have been dead somewhere and I would have never known if Tez didn't tell me. I worry about you every second of every day now, and I keep having these dreams that something bad is going to happen to you, but I'm praying it doesn't because I love you so much." She blinked, and tears fell down her pretty cheeks.

Our waitress came to the table with two menus in her hands. She handed one to me, and the other to Kenosha. "Here you two go. I hope you are enjoying your experience this far?"

I nodded and smiled. "We're good. Just please give us a minute to get our orders together. I'll signal for you when we're ready, if that's okay."

She smiled. "That's perfectly fine." She walked away and stopped at another table in our section a few booths down.

I squeezed Kenosha's hand a little bit. "Baby, I don't want you worrying about me like that, even though I know that ain't fair to ask of you. You know I know how to survive in these streets, and it's the only way we gon' have anything." I rubbed the top of her hand. "I gotta make sure you and our baby is well taken care of at all times. I gotta make sure y'all never need for anything."

She shook her head from right to left. "What about us wanting and needing you to be there, and you can't be because you're dead or locked up? What then, Racine? How am I going to raise a daughter in this world without you? I can't even raise myself without you because you been raising me ever since we were sixteen years old. I fuckin' need you more than I need anybody. And on top of that, I'm pregnant." She lowered her head and snot dripped out of her nose before she sniffed it back up into it.

I felt like the entire world stopped for a minute. I was imagining her having another child in her stomach, and I didn't know what exactly to think right then. My first thought was I had to get my chips all the way up, because two children meant more bills and more money. I was already trying to figure out how I was gon' double the money we'd taken from Rayjon.

She sniffed again. "Baby, can you say something? Because right now you're not saying anything, and it's freaking me out. Do you want me to abort it?"

I felt like I had been slapped by an enemy. I got heated right away. "What? Why you say something like that?"

She cowered. "I don't know, baby. Because you weren't saying anything, and I just thought you were mad at me. I mean, I know we aren't technically together, and I don't know if you wanted another child with me or not. That's all I'm saying. I don't want to lose you, so I'll do whatever you want." Now she was really crying.

I slid around in the booth and wrapped her in my embrace. "Baby, anything we make together, I want us to have it. You're an amazing mother, and I love you. I would never allow you to abort anything that comes out of your body because it belongs to you and me." I kissed her on the forehead. "That just means I gotta go two times harder to make sure our family is straight. I got this. You know I do." I hugged her.

I could feel her still crying against me. "I just don't want you to be mad at me. I don't want you to push me all the way out of your life. I need you, Racine. You're my heart and soul. I swear, you are."

Instead of us going back home after we ate, I decided to take Kenosha to the Sybaris Hotel Suites. I felt like she needed me in a way words wouldn't be able to compensate for. So, as we made it through the door, I tongued her down before picking her up and feeling her wrap her legs around me while I slid the keycard into the slot and walked across the threshold with her sucking all over my neck loudly. "I love you so much, Racine. I'll do anything for you. You're my everything." She continued her sucking, and I kicked the door closed and carried her to the bed, falling onto it on top of her.

I'd chosen the Waterfall Suite, so behind us there was a big slide with water rushing down it, and to the right of the slide was the waterfall. It crashed into the big pool. I could smell the chlorine in the air.

I lay Kenosha all the way back and sat up on my knees. "Baby, I love you, and I appreciate you for bringing our first child into the world. You're an amazing mother, and I honor you, heart and soul. I treasure you, ma." I got to stripping her out of her dress until she was lying on her back in just her red-laced Chanel panties.

She opened her thighs wide as I knelt in between them, sucking on her left inner one. I loved how thick my baby mother was. Before she had Madison, she was kinda slim, but after she gave birth she picked up some weight, and I was in love with her body. I sucked all down her thighs, until I was holding her small right foot in my hand. I kissed the toes on it before doing the same thing to the bottom. "I worship you, baby, and daddy is thankful for you. I'm happy you're having our second child."

She moaned as I sucked her toes into my mouth one at a time, then kissed them individually. "Thank you for saying that, baby. I love you so much."

I sucked back up her calves all the way until I got to her goodie box. Pulling her panties to the side revealing that fat monkey. I put my nose right on it and sniffed. I always loved the scent of my BM's pussy. It took me back to our younger days when all she'd do was let me sniff it up. I smiled at that, peeled her lips back, and kissed her right on the pink before sucking up her juices loudly.

She arched her back and moaned loudly. "Uh! Daddy! Just tell me you love me some more. Please. I need to hear it."

I stuck my tongue as far inside of her as it would go, then licked up and down her crease, sucking her clit into my mouth and nipping it with my teeth. "Daddy loves you, baby. I love you wit' all of my heart." I slurped her jewel back into my mouth and sucked on it hard while my tongue ran from side to side on it. I could feel her juices dripping off my chin. I got to really attacking that pussy a little louder, eating it like there was a gun to my head.

Kenosha threw her head back and started to moan at the top of her lungs, grabbing my head and stuffing it further into her, humping into my face. "Eat me, daddy. Eat me real good. Eat me! Ah!" she screamed and got to humping my face while her juices squirted out of her.

I kept on licking and sucking, slurping up everything that leaked from her pussy. The only thing on my mind was pleasing her and getting her into a better state emotionally. I knew she looked to me to heal her, so I had to stand on my gangsta for her.

She came all over my lips, shaking uncontrollably, then screamed before releasing me from her thighs. I flipped her onto her stomach and opened her thighs before lying on my chest with my face right on her thick ass cheeks. I opened them and let my tongue lick up and down in between those globes before sucking her clit back into my mouth. She started slamming her fist onto the bed, and I reached up and opened her ass wider.

"Uh! Shit. Fuck. Daddy! I love you so much. I'm cumming again. Fuck. I'm cumming again."

I sucked on her clit harder and ran my tongue back across it faster and faster, smacking her on the ass loudly. That caused her to hump into the bed, and she got so wet it felt like she was peeing into my mouth. Her body continued to shake. She reached under herself and spread her pussy lips wider.

After she came again, I flipped her onto her back and kissed her forehead, then all the way down her entire body, telling her how much I loved her and how much I appreciated her for being in my life. I let her know that as long as I had breath in my body, I would make sure her, and our children never needed for anything, and I was dead set on making sure of that.

***

When we got back to my crib the next day, I walked her through the door wit' my arm around her. We were met by Jill sitting in the living room eating a big bowl of oatmeal. When she saw us come through the door wit' smiles on our faces, it looked like her face went through an evil transformation.

"Damn, y'all could have told me you weren't coming back home last night. I been up all night worrying. Kenosha, you ain't get my texts?" she asked, looking salty.

Jill was a chick me and Kenosha allowed to move in wit' her until she could get back on her feet. One of her daughters had been murdered in Chicago a few months back, and she was still picking up the pieces of her life. On top of that, somebody had tried to murder her and her surviving five-year-old daughter, Remy, and she thought it was because she knew the dude who had shot and killed her daughter.

Kenosha shook her head. "To be honest wit' you, I was so wrapped up in Racine that I didn't pay attention to any of that. I was in a weird space last night, and I needed to be healed. I'm sorry and thank you for watching Madison. Where is she?"

Jill nodded. "It's okay, I get it. She's in his bedroom, asleep along wit' Remy. They were up all night watching movies. They might sleep 'til noon."

Kenosha smiled, then walked toward my bedroom, located at the back of the house. Before she disappeared, she turned around. "Racine, thank you, baby. That was all I needed and more. Thank you for making it all about me," she said, then walked away, looking exhausted.

I think she was referring to the fact that the night before I had decided to not put my dick inside of her. I chose to worship her body in every way I could think of, so I used my tongue, my lips, my fingers, and whatever she asked of me. I loved her that much, and I felt like she deserved what I gave her.

As soon I heard my bedroom door close, Jill hopped up, walked over to me, and wrapped her arms around my neck, looking me in the eyes. "Damn, you steady pleasing everybody wit' this dick but me. When is it my turn?" she asked, grabbing my piece and squeezing it. It swelled in her hand, and I couldn't help that shit.

I looked down on her and smiled. "Here you go. You just ain't gon' quit until I hit this pussy, huh?" I reached around and gripped that big-ass booty, massaging it in my hands. I was feeling extra horny because, like I said the night before, I had done everything sexually for Kenosha, so I could heal her, so I didn't get no release. I was feening' for some pussy, and even though I knew I could have gotten it from my BM, I ain't wanna ruin making the healing all about her.

I bent Jill's thick ass over the couch and pulled her purple nightgown up. She was naked underneath, her pussy a little hairy like it hadn't been shaved in a week or so.

She spread her thighs and moaned deep within her throat. "Do it, Racine. Fuck me right now. Please. I'm the only one that ain't got none of that dick yet. It ain't fair."

She ain't have to beg. I was already tearing open the rubber wit' my teeth and sliding it onto my dick before putting the big head up against her sex lips and pushing him in as deep as he would go. I pulled back and slammed him home with force, causing her to yelp. I looked to my right and kept my eye on the door to my bedroom as I fucked her quick and hard while she bounced back into me with her heavy ass cheeks.

"Mm! Mm! Mm! Yes! Mm!" she moaned, slamming back into me so hard I had to grab her hips with aggression just to keep my grip.

That pussy was nice and hot, kinda tight when I first started stabbing it, then it loosened up just a little as I got to work. I was watching the way it jiggled every time I crashed into it. That alone was driving me crazy because Jill was a few pounds away from being a big girl, so everything was jiggling. To me there was nothin' like watching a female's ass and thighs jiggle while I was hittin' that shit.

She grabbed a pillow and bit into. I could hear her screaming as I got to trying to murder that shit. Her pussy sucked at me, then she was shaking, and that caused me to shoot my seed hard.

As soon as I pulled out, I smacked her on that ass. "A'ight, we'll resume this shit at another time. I ain't trying to have Kenosha catch us," I whispered.

Jill was sitting on the floor, still paying wit' her kat and looking up at me with dreamy eyes. "Just promise you gon' hit this shit again. Tell me, Racine. You gon' keep on hitting this shit from time to time, right?" She looked like she was getting ready to cry or something.

I nodded. "I got you, ma. Don't even trip. Just at another time."

She nodded her head slowly and looked optimistic. Even though me and Kenosha wasn't on no one-on-one relationship-type shit, I still didn't want her catching me and Jill in the act. I didn't want her mood to go down.

After I fucked Jill on the couch, I got to feeling guilty as hell. I mean, I knew I wasn't cheating, but I still felt low-down. I jumped into the shower right away and tried to clear my mind.

Chapter 5

I didn't get back up wit' Averie until the next day. She was hearing Rayjon was back out east letting muthafuckas know she had ripped him off, and she was fearing niggaz was about to come at her head, so she wanted to lay low. She hit me up and told me to come and pick up the money and dope before she lost her nerve and gave it back to him. Three hours after the call, I pulled up wit' Tez, and we were sitting on the bed while she paced back and forth in front of us.

"I just don't know, Racine. I'm losing my freaking mind. I know Rayjon. He's crazy. He's going to come for me, and when he does, it ain't gon' be pretty. I don't know what the fuck I was thinking, crossing him," she said, lighting a cigarette.

I had never seen her smoke prior to that day. I could tell she was unraveling at the seams. I stood up and tried to pull her into me, but she jumped and shook her head.

"Not right now. I'm freaking out. You see, because you two don't know him like I do. I know what he's capable of, and you don't. You just fuckin' don't."

She was starting to piss me off a li'l bit. "Yo, you need to calm the fuck down. We can handle this nigga. You making it seem like he bulletproof or somethin'."

"Yeah, fuck that bitch-ass nigga," Tez said, standing up. "I'm tired of hearing you whine and shit. Why the fuck you do all of this if you was gon' be scared and shit?"

Averie stopped in her tracks and mugged Tez. "You know what, Tez? You don't have to good sense God gave a dog. You think everything is a fuckin' joke and you're invincible. Nigga, bullets can kill yo' ass just like they would his. I'm tired of you acting like you so damn macho. You don't know who you dealing wit', so shut up."

Tez frowned. "Bitch, what?"

Before I could even stop him, he snatched her up by the throat and slammed her against the wall, lifting her into the air. She slapped at his hand around her neck, gagging.

"You punk-ass bitch. I'm ti'ed of yo' mouth, anyway. Yo, fuck this ho, Racine. We already got all the paper and the dope. Fuck we need her for?"

I ran over and pulled on his arm. "Yo, nigga, chill. Let her down, cuz. This shit ain't going on like that," I said.

He dropped her to the floor and took a step back. "This bitch is soft, and she gon' be our downfall. She gotta die, Racine. Can't you see this shit?" he asked, mugging me and pointing at her.

Averie coughed loudly and put both of her hands around her neck, crying and gasping for air. "You fucking psycho. I hate you, Tez. You ain't nothin' but a fucking bully. All you do is hurt women."

I saw Tez was getting ready to rush her, so I blocked him. "Yo, chill. I got her, bruh. She just panicking right now."

He mugged me and waved us off. "Fuck that ho. I'll be in the truck, nigga. I can't believe you finna let this soft bitch live. You playin wit' fire." He made his way toward the door, stopped, and looked at me over his shoulder. "This money ours, right?"

I nodded. "Yeah, grab one of them duffels." I watched him do just that before disappearing out of the door.

As soon as he left, I knelt down in front of Averie. "Baby, what's the matter?"

She shook her head slowly. "I'm not built for this shit, Racine. Every second of every day I feel like Rayjon is coming for me. I can't even think straight. I need to get out of here and disappear, and you need to be careful." She stood up, and I did as well. Then she hugged me. "Get yo' weight up, baby, and be ready for that nigga when he comes back, because he's going to come at you hard. That I know for a fact. I need to drop off the radar for a while, but I'll find you when it's time. I hope you can understand that?" she asked, looking into my eyes with a tear running down her cheek.

I nodded. "Do what you gotta do, and when you ready to stand on this throne as queen, it'll be waiting for your presence. Until then, I'm finna build this muthafucking cartel up the right way. Fuck Rayjon. We'll deal wit' that nigga my way."

She stood on her tippy-toes and kissed my lips, then hugged me tight. "I know you an animal, Racine, and I believe in you. Just handle yo' bitness and be smart. When I touch base wit' you again, I wanna see you sitting on a few million since I gave you a million to start wit'. Don't let me down."

I wound up tonguing her down for a li'l while until we went our separate ways. I was surprised she didn't take none of the money from the duffle bags.

She gave me everything, and it fucked my head up because I didn't understand what she saw in me. All I knew was I wasn't gon' fail her.

That same night, me and Tez met up wit' the alderman who ran the district the Robert Taylor Home Projects was in. Tez said we had to sit down wit' him because he had a lot of political pull not only in the real world, but inside of the slums. He said since we were the next crew to take over the projects in his area, we needed to get an understanding.

Back then I didn't know how none of that shit worked. I thought we was just gon' go in there and handle our bitness. Fuck over whatever niggaz in the projects thought they was running shit, and once we cleaned they ass out, take over and get to hustling like crazy because we still had ten kilos of heroin we hadn't even touched yet. They had a Chicago street value of a hunnit thousand apiece. I planned on diming them bitchez up, so we could get every single penny of our profit.

But before we could use all those simple-minded hustling strategies, we had to honor the real world, which said everybody had to answer to somebody else. Even us.

Denzell Robinson was a distinguished gentleman, sixty years old, handsome, and real muscular with naturally-graying curls on his head. He stood about five-foot-ten and kept himself well-dressed in Armani business suits. To the normal eye, he loved looked like a pastor of a church or something, and he even fooled me. That was until we sat down in the den of his big home out in Evanston and he closed the door. Then that hood shit came right out of him.

The first thing he did was set a big bowl of Dro and a box of Cuban cigars on the table in front of me and Tez. "Be my guests, gentlemen, and smoke as much as you want. Get comfortable, because we gon' be here for a minute, or at least until we get an understanding." He sat on the leather seat across from us and took a bottle of champagne out of a bucket of ice before popping the cork.

Shid, I leaned forward and grabbed one of them Cuban cigars and got to breaking that bitch down the middle, while Tez did the same thing. I was finna roll me a blunt so fat that he was gon' wanna put me out, then after I smoked that one I was gon' do it all over again.

Tez started to stuff his blunt before closing it as best he could, and licking the wrap so it stuck together, I wasn't that far behind wit' my own.

"Denzell, I already know that J-Rock an' 'em ain't making you no paper like that. All dem niggaz care about is peanuts and murder, whereas me and my cousin here, we understand the game. We know it's all about money and advancing. I think it's time we weeded them niggaz out, and we did our own thing wit' the Robert Taylors." Tez lit his blunt, took a strong pull, and sat back on the couch.

Denzell poured some of the champagne into a glass, handed the bottle to me, and took a sip from his glass. I drank my champagne straight from the bottle and passed it to Tez, who did the same thing.

Denzell smiled. "You know it's not all about money, although that is important. But what's more important than money is power. You see, as long as you have power, you'll have access to large sums of money. That's a fact." He reached on the side of him and opened a box that already had well-rolled, weed-stuffed Cuban cigars in them. He lit the tip of one of the blunts and inhaled with a smile on his face.

I was high as hell, and when I got high, the main thing on my mind was money. If we were able to take over the Robert Taylors and really get shit going the way it was supposed to, then we could be making damn near two-hunnit thousand a day. Wit' his help and leverage, double that.

"So, what do we have to do in order to fit into yo' grand scheme of things? What's on yo' mind?" I asked, already understanding there would be no way this man would allow us to sit in his home if he didn't already have a game plan for us.

He crossed one of his legs over the other one and took a pull from his blunt, inhaling deeply. "This is the best quality of ganja in Chicago right now. You see, most are smoking weed sprayed wit' roach spray and all other chemicals. But this here is pure. I grow it myself, right in the heart of Havana."

Tez nodded and blew his smoke out. "All that shit is cool, but let's talk bitness. What's good? It's ten project buildings all together that make up yo' district. We wanna take over all of them with no problems, and by 'no problems' I mean from the local authorities. You got pull in high places, we got guns in low places. One hand washes the other. Who are we fucking over to get to where we need to be?" Tez curled his upper lip.

Denzell puffed on his blunt, then took it out of his mouth. "This here is an election year, which means my record will be on display for the last four years I have served. The crime in my area hasn't went down the way it was supposed to, or how I promised it would during my campaign. There is a man by the name of Julian Lewis who is thinking about moving from the eighth district over to mines. He knows I have a larger area, and he'll be looking to have our project buildings torn down, so they can build condominiums. If he does that, our people will be pushed off the south side completely and forced to find affordable housing elsewhere. For most people, the projects are their homes. It might not be the best homes, but in this day and age it's all they have. Julian Lewis doesn't care about the people. He cares about money."

Tez shrugged his shoulders. "So, what, you want us to kill that nigga? No problem. Just say when."

Denzell raised his hand. "Nall, it's more political than that. You see, when one alderman is looking to make a transfer from one district into the next, he must do it by the election of the voters and the higher-ups. All of these people review records and activity from the district you are currently in."

I got it right away and saw where he was going wit' things. "Yo, so you saying you want us to disrupt his district and fill that bitch up wit' bodies. The worse off his reign look on paper, the lesser the chances of him taking over yo' shit."

Denzell made his two fingers into a gun and aimed them at me. "Bingo. Now you're getting it." He took a sip of his champagne. "I don't mind you doing what you have to do by the gun to take over the Taylors, but I want the bodies dropped across Federal Street, because that's his district. I also want you guys in his district fucking shit up. I got a list of drug houses that are sure to bring you large sums of money and dope. All I want is ten percent of all cash, and in exchange for the money I'll keep the local authorities off your ass and let you know when shit is looking like the feds are about to step in. I got blueprints and the whole nine yards. You work wit' me, and I'll work wit' you."

Tez scrunched his face. "What about that nigga J-Rock and his Murda Mafia BDs? Right now, they got control of the Taylors. You already know it's finna be hella bloodshed. How you gon' act about all that in yo' district?"

He smiled. "It won't be in my district because anybody y'all kill, your job is to drop them across State and Federal Street. If you can't make it that far, then you go over to Lewis' district and kill twice as many as you killed in mine. That's the only way."

I sat my blunt in the ashtray. That shit had me high as a muthafucka. I was cool wit' it, but at the same time I was trying to focus in on what they were talking about. "So, in your own estimate: each dope house you sending us to, how much profit is in there?"

He shrugged his shoulders. "I'm sending you to safe houses. None less than a hunnit thousand. After my ten percent, it should be about ninety for you guys, easy. The dope is pure profit. I know it's there, but I don't want any parts of it. Use it to build up the Taylors however you wish, just as long as you're smart. Don't make me look like a fool because if you do, then we'll have to renegotiate some things."

Tez shook his head. "Well, I'm letting you know right now we getting rid of J-Rock an' 'em, and they about forty deep and savages. Luckily, they don't stay in the Taylors. They just hustle out of them, so there won't be as much bloodshed in the buildings. But we gotta do what we gotta do. Far as this list for Julian Lewis goes, let us get that and we'll make one move happen after the next. How many months until the voters start paying attention?"

He laughed. "They already are, so you're going to move fast. And I have some things for you. Come on, follow me."

As soon as I stood up, I felt even higher. It seemed like I was in a movie or something. That bud had me coasting. I smiled at that. We followed him through his house and toward the back of it until we were outside, walking alongside a pool. The cool air woke me up a little bit, but it did nothin' to decrease my high. I was still in the clouds.

After we walked past the pool, I saw we were headed toward the pool house. We were about fifty feet away when this thick-ass, caramel-skinned female stepped out of it wearing some tight Fendi pants that looked as if they had been painted on to her lower half. Up top she wore a sweater that hinted she had some nice titties underneath it, and even from where we were I could tell she was facially fine. She wrapped her arms around herself and shook as if to imply she was freezing.

Denzell walked up to her and wrapped her in his arms, giving her a hug, I wished I could have given her. Trust me, she was that bad.

"Hey, li'l lady. What are you doing back here?" he asked, looking her up and down suspiciously.

She rubbed her own shoulders and looked like she was freezing. "I just put the last of the Christmas ornaments away since I've been asking you to do it for a few weeks now, but you haven't gotten around to it. It'd likely be Valentine's Day had I waited on you." She rolled her eyes. "And who might they be?" she asked, looking at me real weird like.

Denzell rolled his head around on his neck, then took a step back and began to introduce us. "Janine, this is Tez, and this here –"

"Racine! Oh my God, I know that ain't you all grown up?" She moved Denzell out of the way by nudging past him, then stood in my face, holding my cheeks with her small, gloved hands.

I felt awkward as hell. I didn't think I knew who this broad was, though she was fine, so I was trying to determine whether we'd gotten together back in the day or somethin'. "May I ask who you are?"

She bucked her head backward as if she were offended. "It's me, Ms. Robinson."

I gave her a crazy look that should have let her know I still couldn't place the relation.

She sighed out loud, and mist came from her mouth because of the cold. "From third grade. I was your teacher, and you used to drive me crazy. Fighting all the time. Always kissing on the girls and trying to look up my dress. You were a horrible child."

I bucked my eyes and looked her from head to toe, amazed. Damn, I could not believe that was her. Even though I was only in the third grade back then,

I used to have a thing for her. I could not believe she had kept herself together the way she had. She was bad. I thought she might have been just a few years older than me and Tez, not way, way older. "Damn, you look great," I said before I could stop myself.

She blushed and lowered her head. "Thank you." She looked up into my eyes and didn't say a word for a few seconds. I could tell she was choosing, though. She looked like she wanted to eat me alive, and I would have enjoyed that fate. Damn, I couldn't believe how bad she was.

Denzell must have peeped the atmosphere and decided to break that shit up. "Well, it's good y'all know each other. Now you get your ass in that house, and you come wit' me."

We did just as he said, but before we disappeared into the pool house I looked over my shoulder and caught a glimpse of Janine's fat-ass booty. That muthafucka was out and jiggling every time she walked. Her thighs were thick, too. I felt myself getting hard and had to focus in on something else.

After we got into the pool house and sat down, Denzell came out of the back dragging a big green trunk. "One of you young boys wanna help me carry this before my back go out?" he asked.

Me and Tez both jumped up and wound up carrying it to the spot below the aquarium that he pointed to. Once there, he came over and knelt down, unlocking it and opening the trunk all the way up.

I got to looking around the pool house and could not believe how nice it looked inside. The place was all white, including the leather couches and pool table. There was a bar inside of it with plenty of liquor of all kinds and what looked to be a seventy-inch smart screen television. I nodded my head in approval and knew I would have all that one day real soon. I turned my attention back to the trunk just as Denzell grabbed an AR.15 out of it and handed it to Tez.

"Hell yeah! I like this muthafucka right here," he said, looking it over.

"You should. It holds fifty shots in its magazine, and it spits rapidly. You tap the trigger and it shoots three bullets at a time. It's highly accurate, and there is even a green beam on the top of its scope. This whole trunk is filled with them, and ammunition. You'll owe me twenty grand for them, when you get it. Keep in mind, that's not including my ten percent. Do we understand each other?"

I knelt in front of the trunk and looked it over. I already knew what kind of shit we could do wit' that kind of artillery. "Bet, you'll have that twenty gees by the end of the day."

"Yeah. Now, what's good wit' that hit list?" Tez asked.

Denzell nodded his head and laughed briefly. "I will most definitely be in touch. We'll do a step-by-step, but by the shaking of my hand, that means we are in business together." He extended his hand to Tez, and they shook before he did the same thing to me.

Chapter 6

Before we could even get started taking over the Taylors, some other beef woke the fires of me and Tez's past. It was three days after we had the sit-down wit' Denzell, and Tez was feeling like taking a load off and just kicking back for a day or so, which I thought was cool because I wanted to spend some time with Madison. The two days prior, me and Tez, along wit' Wayne and E, had spent bagging up heroin. I wanted to have two whole kilos aluminum-foiled and bagged up before we got to hustling out of the Taylors, so that's what we were doing when Tez decided he wanted to hit up the Matrix, a well-known night club all the ballers in the city hit up every weekend. It was basically a fashion show, and if you weren't dressed fresh or pulled up driving something foreign, they didn't even let you in the door.

After he told me what he had on his mind, I decided to rent a 2019 Jaguar SRJ, all black, with the all-red leather interior. Tez copped the all-red one with the all-black interior, and we each had one of the li'l homies roll in the passenger seats of the whips. That nigga E rolled wit' me because, for some reason, we just jammed a little harder. Plus, he was quick to bust his gun, just like I was. Birds of a feather, I guess.

Anyway, I got fitted in and all-black-and-red Eves St. Laurent fit wit' the Diadora shades and the matching St. Laurent boots. I ain't really fuck wit' jewelry because I was a jack-boy myself, and I always felt like niggas who wore jewelry was just advertising to be robbed, so I ain't rock none this night, either. My only jewelry was the .45 taped to my inner thigh.

We stepped into the club after being patted-down by some fat-ass nigga that smelled like cologne and musk. I hated when people put cologne or deodorant on over their dirty bodies. That shit was not meant to make a nigga smell better if they were already funky. It was designed to keep them smelling up to par, but a nigga already had to be there.

Once we got past him, I looked out into the club as Tez put his arm around my shoulder. "Nigga, I'm finna fuck at least two of these thick-ass hoez that's walking around her. Look at these bitchez. Damn!" Tez said, shaking his head.

It seemed like everywhere I looked there were groups of females dancing with other females. Most of them were strapped and had skirts on so short their asses and thighs were out. And these weren't no average, run-of-the-mill-looking females. Nall, these broads were fine and got my stamp of approval.

"Cuz, on some real shit, we needed this. I ain't been out in a while," I said as the DJ played a song by Money Bags Yo.

The dance floor was crowded, and the club was lit up with all different kinds of lights flashing on and off. Way across the floor and to the other side of the big club was the VIP section. It was closed off wit' velvet ropes and three beefy-ass security guards. I already knew I was about to make my way over there.

The music seemed to get louder. "Look, cuz, I'm finna go mingle. Wayne gon' stay wit' me. You keep E wit' you, and I'll meet you in the VIP section in about thirty minutes. Luv, nigga," Tez said.

"Yep." I waved for E to follow me and we made our way through the crowd to the VIP section. I hated brushing across so many people. That always annoyed me, but it was the only way to get to our destination.

We were about halfway there when a real fine Puerto Rican-lookin' chick tried to scoot past me wit' two drinks in her hand. She was cole, with long, curly hair that dropped to her stomach. She was short, about five feet even and small up top, but had plenty of hips and ass, just like I liked them. I didn't know where she was planning on going before I spotted her, but I was about to make her take a detour.

As she tried to wiggle past me, I stepped in front of her and held out my hand. "How you doing, li'l momma? My name is Racine."

She looked me up and down, then smiled before sucking on her bottom lip all sexy-like. "My name is Ellie. I'm from Crown Town and trying to get these drinks over to my sister, who is sitting right there," she said, pointing with one of the drinks in her hand.

I looked across the dance floor and saw another badass Puerto Rican broad sitting at a table wit' her head down. "Yo, she look kinda sad. Maybe y'all should join me and my mans in the VIP section in about five minutes. Maybe we can help you cheer her up."

Ellie shrugged her shoulders. "Is cool wit' me. So, what, we should just come over and they'll move the rope? I hope so, because I'm not paying five hundred dollars just to sit in another part of the club. No, thank you."

I laughed. "Yeah, that's cool. Just meet me over there. I'll pay for everything, including y'all drinks. Just tell yo' sister the night is on me."

Ellie smiled and sucked on her bottom lip again. "Okay, I'll do that. But I want you for myself, so when she comes over, let your guy get at her, not you." She walked off, and her dress was so tight it hugged her big ass. I mean it looked like her ass was a pregnant stomach or something.

I made my way to the VIP section just as E stepped beside me holding a bottle of Grey Goose. As soon as security saw us standing by the ropes, he came over and looked me up and down. I didn't like that, and I wanted to get at him, but Ellie crossed my brain. I had to get to know shorty that night.

"Five hunnit to cross this rope, four people or less. Y'all want in?" he asked with sweat glistening on the top of his head.

I peeled off five $100 bills and handed them to him. "Look, we got those two females right there that's wit' us. When they come, just let 'em through."

He nodded, then a dark-skinned waitress came over with a menu. "What you ballas sipping on? We got everything-top-of-the-line, however you want it," she said, licking her cherry lips.

I looked her up and down and had to give her props. She had a swagger about her I had to appreciate. "Just bring me a bottle of Hennessy and a bottle of Ace of Spades. When those ladies right there come through the ropes, you take their orders and give them whatever they want."

She licked her juicy lips again. "Damn, my nigga, you holding paper like that? Maybe I should just quit and come sit on yo' lap. I'm pretty sure it's enough room for me," she flirted, battin' her fake eyelashes.

I smiled, then got serious. "Shorty, wit' all that ass, you can come sit on my lap at anytime, and I'll put you up on yo' own paper."

She bit into her bottom lip and looked me over for a long time, not saying a word, just looking. "You know what? I just might take you up on that offer. Let me think it over." She walked away, and I noted how tight her black biker pants were. It showcased her entire frame from the waist down.

Me and E settled into our booth as Ellie and her sister came through the rope and slid in beside us, wit' Ellie on my right and her sister to the left of me. They both smelled good and looked even better.

"Racine, this my sister, Mardi. Her husband just got sentenced to life in prison yesterday and it's killing her. I hope y'all can help me cheer her up. Mardi, this is Racine and his guy, um. Um. I'm sorry, I never got your name, Papi. What is it?"

"My name E, ma, and it's nice to meet both of y'all. Sorry to hear about yo' nigga. I already know that's hard. Anything you need, just let me know," he said.

"Thank you, guys. You know what? E, if you don't mind, I'd like to dance a little bit to take my mind off things for a bit."

"Nall, that sound good to me. Come on," he said, and I watched them disappear onto the dance floor.

I turned to Ellie and got to eating her up wit' my eyes. "So, what's good wit' you, baby?"

She blushed and looked away. "You're so damn handsome. I ain't never had a dude as good looking as you approach me with respect. I'm wondering, what's your angle? Are you some kind of player or something?"

I laughed. "N'all, I ain't no player, and I ain't got no angles. I just wanna chill. I saw you, you looked bad to me, crushing every other female in here, so I figured why waste my time out there trying to search for a woman as cole as you are when you were smack dead in my face already. I'm fulfilled. Now I wanna get to know you. What are your intentions for the night?"

She shrugged her shoulders. "I don't know. Like I said before, I just wanted to bring my sister out to take her mind off everything that happened wit' her husband. Well, he wasn't really her husband, but they had been together for a few years, and the fact he will never walk the streets again is killing her. So, I figured maybe we'd go out a meet some guys who could at least take us away from our realities." She shrugged her shoulders. "I don't know, but it seems like it's working," she said, looking out at the dance floor.

Mardi had her arms around the top of E's neck. They grooved on the dance floor to a Remy Ma track. "Well, you told me what yo' sister reality is, so what's yours?" I asked, scooting a little closer to her and grabbing the bottle of Ace. "Can I pour you some of this champagne?"

She grabbed an empty glass off the table and held it out for me to pour the liquid into. "Thank you." She tossed her long, curly hair back over her shoulder. "Um, my reality is I barely have any time for anything. I work sixty hours a week most times as a nursing assistant, and I'm also being trained at the police academy over on Cottage Grove on my downtime. I'm thinking about becoming a cop. That way I can know for sure there is at least one good one working in the city of Chicago."

Her saying that she wanted to be a cop was throwing me for a loop, especially since I knew how I got down. I tried to imagine her dressed up in a police uniform, and I was having a hard time doing so. She was too pretty for that. "Why a cop?" I asked, sipping from the bottle.

She lowered her head and sat her glass back on the table. She was quiet for a long time, then took a deep breath and exhaled loudly. "My younger brother was killed by two white cops over on Halstead two summers ago. He was a good kid, never got into any trouble, and they shot him down in the street. They say it was mistaken identity. My mom sued, and there is supposed to be a settlement, but for me it's just not enough. My heart is still broken." She swallowed, lowered her head even further downward, and started to cry.

I put my arm around her and pulled her head to my chest. "It's okay, Ellie. You just have to be strong. I'm here for you in any way you need me to be," I said, holding her close. I could only imagine how she was feeling. The police in Chicago were dirty as hell. Not only would they gun yo' ass down and take yo' body and drop it off in a rival's territory to make it seem as if your enemy had murdered you, but they were the worst when it came to sexually assaulting females.

I wanted to ask Ellie what she planned on doing once she became apart of the force, but E came back into our VIP section with a look of anger on his face. Mardi followed close behind.

"Bruh, we gotta get over there to Tez. Them bitch-ass Lords from out west got him boxed in. I'm ready to start busting in this muthafucka," he said, clenching his jaw.

I hopped up, ready to go to my cousin's aid. "Let's go, bruh. We definitely ain't about to let that shit pop off."

I was on my way out of the section when Ellie grabbed my arm. "Wait, Racine. Here, at least take my phone number." She touched her phone to the back of my I-phone eleven. "Make sure you get up wit' me. You have a nice spirit."

By the time I got to the front of the club where Tez was, he was in a crowd full of grimy-looking niggaz with long, nappy dreads. Before I got over there, I sent E out the back door and told him to be ready to wet any one of them niggaz as they exited the club if I texted him a nine-eleven to his phone. That was code for aid and assistance.

When I found Tez, he was stuck in the circle of niggaz with his face frowned-up. "You niggaz think I'm gon' fold because it's a bunch of you studs? Nigga, this ain't that. Fuck you niggaz wanna do?" he said, adjusting the Ferragamo belt on his waist.

One of the niggaz had a bottle of Moet in his hand. He poured the liquor out onto the floor and turned the bottle upside down. I felt like that nigga was finna hit my cousin in his head wit' that bottle, and I don't even think Tez peeped his move because he was in the middle of the pack. I was wondering why the security ain't come over and see what was going on. They weren't on shit, which meant I had to be. I reached deep down in my pants and pulled my pistol from the tape I had around it and my thigh. As soon as it came loose, I turned it upside down and forced my way into the circle just as the nigga wit' the Moet bottle was trying to creep Tez. I got to him before he got to my cousin, reached back, and brought the pistol forward so fast and hard right against the side of his face. *Crack!*

"Bitch-ass nigga, shit ain't sweet!"

The side of his face busted open and started bleeding before he even hit the ground. I turned the gun around and aimed that bitch at all of them niggaz because they looked like they were finna bum-rush my ass. "I'll pop any one of you bitch-ass niggaz. Just try me, blood."

They jumped back, and even a few ducked down as Tez reached deep into his pants and pulled up his .45 pistol, aiming at them niggaz. "Bitch-ass niggaz, what's hannen'?" he hollered with his gun turned sideways.

The niggaz started to disburse, running every which way. Since they were running, it was like the other people in the club started to panic. I could hear females screaming and the sounds of glass breaking. Tables were knocked over, and I felt like it was time for me and Tez to get up out of there. I didn't know where Wayne was at the time, and I didn't have the time to look for him. I sent E the nine-eleven text, and put my phone back in my pocket, smacking Tez on the shoulder. "Come on, nigga. Let's go."

71

The crowd was going crazy, and I couldn't really tell who was who, or where them niggaz had went. All I knew was in Chicago it was easy for you to get yo' shit blew off when everybody was running out of the club hysterical, because it created so much chaos a shooter could easily get a few shots in if they wanted to.

When we made it outside, it was just like I thought it was gon' be: snowing, and somehow a couple of them niggaz had made it to their whips first and were parked in front of the door, waiting on us. As soon as I came through the door, I saw the tinted window to an all-gold Cadillac Escalade lower, and then the nose of an AK-47 came out of it. Tez was right behind me. I turned around and tackled him to the ground just as the shots started.

Boom, boom, boom, boom, boom, boom, boom, boom! "That's them niggaz right there, Lord. Hit they ass, nigga!" *Boom, boom, boom, boom, boom!*

A bunch of people that were still standing screamed. I felt some hot liquid splash onto my face, and then a female fell on me, holding her neck. I watched another dude get stood-up by the bullets before he fell backward with multiple holes in him.

Tez lay on his back and gripped his pistol wit' both hands, aiming at the truck. *Doom! Doom! Doom! Doom! Doom!* His bullets slammed into the body of the truck just as it sped away, kicking up snow under its tires. It hit a crowd of people.

More screaming ensued before Wayne ran across the parking lot with a pump in his hands. *Boom! Boom! Boom!* His bullets shattered the truck's back window. I heard a nigga holler out inside of it. He must've hit the driver because instead of the truck moving, it stayed still. The doors opened and four niggaz jumped out and started to run.

Boom! Boom! Boom! "Let's get the fuck out of here, bruh!" Wayne said, waving us over.

Doom! Doom! I watched E jump out from between some cars and catch one of the runners slipping. He popped him twice and stomped him in the chest. He looked across the parking lot at another one of them and busted his gun. *Doom! Doom! Doom!* This runner fell as well. Two shots slammed into his back, knocking him forward.

I'll never forget that night because it was the night we accrued some real long-lasting enemies who would later threaten our empire.

Chapter 7

The next day after that shit had taken place, I decided it would be smart for us to lay low for a week or so, then we would get back on our project business. I wanted to spend some time wit' Kenosha, seeing as she was pregnant and all. The next day, instead of leaving out the crib, I chose to lay in bed with her, hugged up.

She lay on my chest, rubbing my abs, and every now and then she would kiss them. "You know what, Racine? I'm a little scared to have this baby," she said, looking up at me.

I was rubbing her thick thighs, and every so often I'd squeeze her ass. She was lying on her side, and I couldn't resist doing just that. Kenosha was nice and strapped, and ever since she'd had Madison, I'd had a thing for her body. I think I just appreciated it more after knowing she brought our daughter into this world.

"Baby, what are you afraid of?" I asked, watching the news on our big screen. I had it on subtitles wit' no sound on. They were still talking about the shooting at the Matrix from the night before.

She squeezed my stomach muscles, then ran her hand up to my chest, rolling her finger around my brown nipple. "I'm scared somethin' gon' happen to you and I'm gon' wind up raising our two children on my own. Every time you leave out of this house, I just feel like I'm never going to see you again. It's starting to take a toll on me," she said softly.

I really didn't feel like getting into one of these kinds of conversations. Kenosha had been wit' me ever since we were, like, fifteen. I had always been a street nigga. I couldn't understand why all the sudden she was having these daily, worrisome breakdowns. "Baby, I don't wanna talk about that shit. Look, I'm here wit' you right now, and I'm alive and well. That's all that should matter."

There was a knock on the door. "Who is it?" Kenosha asked, sounded like she was irritated.

"It's Jill. Are y'all busy right now?"

The way shit was going wit' Kenosha, I already knew she was about to get to kicking all kinds of knowledge and telling me why she was worried and all that shit. I just didn't feel like hearing that. "N'all, come on in, Jill. The door open."

Kenosha raised her head and shot daggers at me. "Damn. Okay."

Jill opened the door wearing some tight denim capris that made her thighs look extra right. I found myself looking at them before I even looked into her face. I could see her camel toe and everything in them jeans, and I was remembering how good her pussy was. I felt my dick twitch.

"Uh, I just got my food share card in the mail and I wanted throw a little food in the house, if that's okay. Racine, can you give me a ride to Aldi's?"

Now, my intentions were to stay in the house and chill wit' Kenosha, but I could tell where things were headed with her. Madison and Remy were in school, which meant my only escape would have to be Jill. And being honest, it wasn't a bad one, either.

Before Kenosha could say anything, I jumped up and got fitted in Polo. "Yo, you want me to grab you anything specific from the store, or you good?" I asked Kenosha.

She climbed out of the bed and I noted her little purple panties were all up in her sex lips. Those panties looked like they were too small for her, especially when she turned around and I saw how her brown cheeks were bare. They swallowed her panties whole. She was definitely getting thicker.

She waved us off. "Nall, I'm good. Y'all just don't be all damn day, because I wanna finish talking to you, Racine. I feel like it's important." I walked over to her and tried to kiss her on the forehead, but she moved her face. "I don't feel like that shit right now. Just get yo' ass back here."

I got a little irritated, but I wasn't finna argue wit' her right then.

Me and Jill didn't even make it three blocks over before she was pulling my dick out of my Ralph Laurens and deep throatin' me while she moaned around it. I immediately pulled over and let my seat all the way back and enjoyed her head game. She sucked me so hard and fast I had to close my eyes because it was feeling so good.

She popped me out of her mouth with a loud sucking noise. "I been wanting to taste this big-ass dick ever since you pulled it out of me. I want you to cum in my mouth, so I can know what you taste like. Please, Racine. I'm begging you." She popped me back in and got to sucking me harder while she pumped her fist up and down my shit.

I got to rising out of my seat, going deeper into her mouth, imagining the way Kenosha's panties were stuck all in her sex lips. Then I imagined what it felt like to have Jill bent all over the couch wit' her ass jiggling, and before I knew it I was cumming in thick globs all down her throat while she moaned her approval and kept on sucking.

I reached down and pulled a Magnum out of my pocket, opened it wit' my teeth, and gave it to her. "Put this muthafucka on my shit and get yo' thick ass up here and ride this dick. Hurry up!"

She put the condom into her mouth and rolled it down my dick before straddling me and sliding down my pole. I felt that hot pussy searing my dick, sucking at it as it ate it inch-by-inch until she took it all with her eyes rolled into the back of her head. "Uh! Shit. Now let me fuck this dick the way it's supposed to be fucked." She humped forward hard. "Aw!" She rolled her back and humped forward again. "Aw!" And again. "Aw! Aw! Aw! Uh! Shit! Um! Yes! Yes! Oh, this dick!" She wrapped her arm around my neck and started to really ride me.

I gripped that big ass and forced her to take my shit roughly, pulling her shirt up and exposing them big, brown titties with the huge nipples on them. They were erect, and I sucked them into my mouth while she rode me, moaning into my ear.

After we got done doing the do and grocery shopping, we got back to the crib. Before we opened the door to my truck, Jill leaned over and kissed me on the lips at the same time Kenosha was opening the door. It was like that shit happened just, so Kenosha could go ballistic, which is just what she did.

She ran down the steps and pulled open Jill's door, then reached in and grabbed her by her micro braids, dropping her to the snow while Jill tried to figure out what the hell was going on.

"You shysty bitch. I knew you just wanted to get my baby daddy alone, so you could make a move on him. All you talk about is Racine. I should have known what you were up to." She dragged her on the snow, then punched her right in the jaw three times with Jill's braids wrapped around her right wrist.

Jill got to kicking her legs and trying to break away, but it was to no avail. Kenosha had been a scrapper all her life, or for as long as I had known her. She had Jill's braids securely wrapped around her right hand and wrist, so she could fuck her up wit' her left hand. Kenosha was left-handed.

I jumped out of the truck and made my way over to the pair. As soon as I got close enough, Kenosha held up her left hand, stopping me. "Racine, don't get involved in this shit because it ain't got nothin' to do wit' you yet. Let me handle my womanly bitness. I'll deal wit' yo' low-down ass later."

As much as I hated to, I had to respect her gang-sta, so I just got to grabbing bags out of the car while she whooped Jill's ass. She pushed her to the ground and straddled her, slapping her across the face again and again before punching her in the nose, busting her shit. Blood dripped down her cheeks and turned the snow red underneath them. "Trifling bitch. I let you stay in my house, and all you want is my baby daddy dick. I hate you kind of hoez. Here a bitch is trying to help you out, and you looking for a way to betray her." She slapped the shit out of her again.

Jill spit blood across the snow. "I'm not gon' fight you, Kenosha, because I was wrong. So, whoop my ass. Whoop it good, because I'm sorry," she cried.

Kenosha slapped her across the face again, then stood up. "You stupid bitch. I should kick yo' ass out. You lucky you got Remy. If you didn't, you'd be out in them streets in the fuckin' cold." She turned around and walked up the steps, pulling me by the shirt. "Let me holla at you, Racine."

I moved her hand up off me and followed her into the house, but before I went inside I looked over my shoulder and saw Jill struggling to get up. I felt bad for her. I knew we were bogus and shit was just as much my fault as it was hers. She was just so damn thick. That was my weakness.

As soon as I stepped into the living room, Kenosha smacked the shit out of me. I mean she smacked me so hard I had to take a step back. I balled up my fist, about to bust her in her shit, but caught myself.

"Go 'head, Racine. Hit me! I don't give a fuck no more." Tears ran down her face. "How dare you leave the house just so you can fuck this bitch when I was laying in the bed wit' you ass-naked. What? You prefer this bitch pussy to mines now?" She looked sick.

I took a deep breath and tried to calm down. My face was on fire. I was heated and felt like killing somethin'. "Look, Kenosha, it ain't even like that. You overreacting like a muthafucka. Me and Jill was just —" She stepped forward and swung at me, but I ducked her punch, then came up and wrapped her into my arms.

"Nigga, don't even lie to me and say you ain't fucked that bitch. Yo' truck smell just like her pussy. That's why I whooped her ass. Let me go!" she hollered and twisted in my grasp.

I wasn't finna lie to her because I never felt like I needed to. I felt like she was overreacting because she knew her, and I wasn't in no monogamous relationship. We had never established that. "I wasn't finna say that, but you need to calm yo' li'l ass down, because if you hit me again, Kenosha, I'm gon' hit yo' ass back." I didn't know if I would, but she was definitely pushing my limits.

She jerked out of my grasp, turned around, and mugged me. "Tell me if you like fucking that bitch more than me. Tell me she suck you better than I can, and I'll let y'all do y'all," she hollered with anger written across her pretty face.

"What?" I frowned. "Man, stop playin' wit' me. You my first love. Ain't nobody got shit on you. It's just fuckin', Kenosha. Damn. You and her did it!"

"Racine," Kenosha began before we were interrupted.

Jill ran into the living room with a worried look on her face. "Kenosha, yo' momma out here shaking on the ground. Her face all beat up and everything."

"What?" Kenosha ran past me and outside with me right behind her.

It had started to snow again, and the wind picked up speed, lowering the temperature. The sun began to set. When I looked down the stairs, I saw Janet, Kenosha's mother, was lying in the snow on the concrete. She was shaking with blood pouring out of her mouth. Her head was twice its normal size, and she appeared to be thirty pounds skinnier than when I had seen her last.

Kenosha ran down the steps and fell down the last three before hopping up and running to her mother's side. While I was worried about Janet, I was even more worried about our child inside of Kenosha's stomach.

She started to cry right away as Janet started to shake harder. "Momma! Momma! Who did this to you? Who did this?"

I came over and looked down on Janet, then looked both ways for any signs of enemies. I didn't know what she had gotten involved in, but whoever had done it had obviously known where her daughter laid her head. I was gon' have to change all that shit up real fast.

Janet continued to shake. She looked like she wanted to say something, but only coughed up a bunch of blood before having a seizure and dying in Kenosha's arms.

Kenosha's eyes got bucked, then she started to scream. "No! Mommy, please, don't go!"

We buried her four days later at the church around the corner from Kenosha's crib. It was still a mystery what had happened to her, but I figured we'd find out when the time was right.

Kenosha took her death hard. She stopped eating and everything. She mostly stayed inside of her bedroom in silence. I stayed in that bed right wit' her, tending to her every need. I think I might've kissed her on the forehead a million times in two weeks, but I knew it was what she needed. I fed her, bathed her, and told her I loved her, and she would never be alone. It took her about nine days to get ahold of herself, and I made sure I was by her side every single day.

Tez hit me up on the tenth day saying Denzell had given us our first mission and he needed me by his side ASAP! I hung up the phone wit' him and turned to Kenosha, who was still snuggled up in my arms. I was trying to find a way to let her know I had to get back out into them streets, so I could be on bitness, but I really didn't have to because she understood the game for the most part.

"Racine, I already know you gotta get back out there. You been under me for ten days straight, and I appreciate you more than you know, but you being in here ain't getting us ahead in life, so you gotta be out there. But I'll just say this, baby: remember I am here pregnant with your second child, and whatever decisions you make out there will deeply affect your family. I need – we need you, and we love you," she said, rubbing her stomach and looking me in the eyes.

I leaned down and kissed her on her juicy lips, then leaned back to look into her pretty, freckled face. "I got this, baby. I know I fuck up at times, but I'm getting it together. While I'm out here in these streets, I want you to be online and lookin' for a house out in Evanston or something. A whole house, too. Ain't no more of this apartment shit. I gotta upgrade my babies. And if it's anything else you feel like you need, get that, too, and I'll pay for it. From here on out I gotta do a better job at taking care of you and making sure you know you are appreciated, because I can never thank you enough for being a mother to our children or for being as stomp-down as you are. You are a queen, and I honor you, boo."

Tears rolled down her cheeks. She crawled to me and wrapped her arms around my neck. "I love you so much, Daddy. I don't know what I would do without you. You're my everything."

I held her for a while, rubbing her back, falling deeper in love with the queen who was my children's mother, knowing I had to get better as a man to show her she was first in my life.

Chapter 8

"Denzell want us to drive up the murder rate a li'l bit over in Julian Lewis district. The gangstas over there supposed to be having some kind of block party and picnic for a bunch of they new members that they just recruited. At the same time, they celebrating them, they making it look like they doing somethin' for the people. Denzell said shit ain't gon' look right if this party go off wit'out a hitch because the gangstas in his district supposedly don't bow down to nobody, so if it looks like they are throwing a block party for the people and feeding everybody, it's gon' look like Julian Lewis got them to fall in line and take care of the community instead of harming it like they been doing. So, what we gotta do is go over there and disrupt some shit," Tez said, sitting down at the table in his basement before picking up and AR-15 and slamming a clip into it.

It was only one o'clock in the afternoon the same day me and Kenosha had gotten an understanding, and I was trying to find out as much as I possibly could about this move before we made it. E and Wayne sat around the table as well, loading up their assault rifles with red bandanas around their hands. They listened on nonchalantly as if everything Tez was saying didn't affect them at all.

I slid the latex gloves on my hands and grabbed an AR-15, lookin' it over before slamming a hunnit-round clip inside of it and cocking it on the side. "Cuz, it's gon' be plenty women and kids at this block party. I don't give a fuck what Denzell talking about. I'm not hitting none of them, my nigga, and y'all ain't, either. Let's get that shit established right now." I got to thinking about Madison and Kenosha going to a block party thinkin' they were just going to have a good time, then some niggas like us came and wet that bitch up, hitting them and other defenseless people like them for no reason. I wasn't going for that. Just that thought alone was about to make me call this move off.

Tez shook his head, then stood up, looking through the scope of his assault rifle. "That's what we got scopes for, li'l cuz. We know who we gotta hit. I think that's perfectly clear, but just on some real shit, I'm gon' handle my bitness no matter what. I ain't going over there trying to dodge muthafuckas. If they jump in my line of fire, I'm poppin' they ass, too, and life goes on."

Wayne smiled, exposing the gold teeth in his mouth. "That's how I feel. A kill is a kill. If I wind up knocking off the heads of a few kids or a couple bitchez, it is what it is. Shit, it's already set in stone when a muthafucka gon' die, anyway."

I could tell this nigga was high as hell because he wasn't making no sense. Neither one of them fools were. I wasn't wit' this shit they was talking about. It was getting me heated a li'l bit, too, especially once I got to thinking about how Jill's li'l daughter got kilt by a bunch of reckless shooting. The bullet wasn't even meant for her.

E shook his head. "Y'all better do the best y'all can, then, 'cause I ain't on that dumb shit. Killing them weak-ass niggaz ain't shit to me, but we getting to hitting up women and kids, then they gon' try and call that shit a terrorist attack and hunt our ass down.

Fuck that. I'm trying to be hood rich, my nigga. We can't be that if we constantly on the ropes because of the Feds. Let's just hit every nigga who look like he banging and stay away from the females and kids, that simple." He put his rifle down and stuck his hand into a bag of Doritos before crunching on about four at one time.

I liked that fat nigga because it was like we were always on the same page. "I agree wit' li'l homie. Let's just handle dis bitness the smart way, then we can focus on the Taylors for the next few weeks and that nigga J-Rock an' 'em. That's what's important."

Tez was quiet for a short while, then lay his hand on Wayne's shoulder. "Look, li'l homie, they got a point. As much as I don't give a fuck about a bitch or one of them snotty-nosed-ass kids, obviously they do, so just try and knock them blue niggaz's heads off and leave the bitchez and kids alone. You feel me?"

Wayne shrugged his shoulders. "Yeah. I mean, orders are orders."

After we put our game plan in place, we went and ordered a pizza from the Home Run Inn. I felt it was imperative for us to bond as homies before we went out into that battle field. It wasn't all about shooting up shit when it came down to forming a crew of savages. There had to be love and respect there. Even though we were all killas, it was important for us to have an emotional bond, because when the money started to roll in, had a bond not been formed between all members, greed would set in and slowly destroy yo' mob. Greed was the number one poison in most crews.

"Yo, after we done hitting this lick, I wanna take you li'l niggas to the car lot and let y'all pick a few whips. Ain't no reason for me and Tez to be rolling nice and y'all out here braving the elements wit' no whips. Not only that, but for now I'ma put five bands apiece in yo' pockets just so you can get a feel of having that type of paper. This here is a family, and we gotta start to move as such," I said, looking around the table at E and Wayne as they attacked their meal.

Tez nodded. "Yeah, I'm wit' that. All my killaz gotta look fresh out here in these streets. That's what make out cartel look appealing. I feel like we need about four mo' niggaz, too. They gotta be starving, hungry for that paper, and bred wit' loyalty."

Wayne swallowed his mouthful of pizza and drank from his glass of pop. "I wanna have my li'l brothers get down wit' us, too. They twins, and they 'bout that action just like I am. Right now, they fucking around in Moe Town wit' them stone niggaz, and I don't like that shit. I feel like if they gon' be busting they gun, they should be doing that shit for our cause. The Moes paying them peanuts."

"A'ight. Well, we'll review that shit a little later. Right now, let's make this bitness happen so we can focus on the Taylors. It's time to get our weight up," I said, wiping my hands on a napkin.

We waited until about three o'clock before we rode out to the block party. The sun had come out, and thankfully it wasn't as cold as it had been over the last few weeks. I had that nigga E wit' me. He sat in the passenger seat chewing his gum and nodding his head to the Money Bags Yo that was bangin' out of my speakers. I don't know what was on his mind, but I was just hoping everything went off without a glitch.

I parked four blocks down from the block party in an alley on State Street, right inside of an abandoned garage, and me and E got out carrying duffle bags with our rifles inside of them. I know that shit had to look suspicious as hell, and I was hoping it didn't bring any attention to us. But the way Chicago was set up, everybody was always trying to sell something, so it was a few people out wit' duffle bags.

When we got a block away we could hear the loud music, and I saw the streets were blocked off. We unloaded our weapons from inside another abandoned garage. My heart was beating fast, and I was trying to psyche myself up to do what I had to do. I had never been in any drama wit' none of them gangsta niggaz, and it was hard trying to get into a mindset where I was ready to kill them up. I know a lot of niggaz make that killing shit seem easy, but in real life it takes a lot to process anger in order to kill.

E rolled his mask down his face. "I hate these niggaz over here anyway, Jo. Every time I cross Federal Street they get to busting at me for no reason. These niggaz and them fools from Vulture City. Payback is a bitch." He looked me over. "You ready?"

I rolled my mask down and thought, *fuck it*, I had to do what I had to do. I was in the life, and since I was, I had to handle my bitness. "Remember, no women and kids, li'l homie. Aim for them niggaz."

He nodded. "I got you, Jo."

We ran out of the garage and split up. I ran alongside the garage and into the backyard of the house it was sitting behind before coming out on the corner. It was mostly deserted wit' people heading for the block party taking place one block over. I looked to my right and saw Tez already running across the street and alongside another house, headed toward the block party. That made me put a little pep in my step. Then I was running, crossing the street, alongside another house, through the alley, another backyard, then I crouched down on the side of a house on the same block as the party.

The music was super loud at this point. I could hear a crowd of people. It sounded like they were enjoying themselves. I got a little closer, looked out into the street, and saw a bunch of children playing with their big coats on, chasing each other while a bunch of adults were barbecuing. Others were talking and kicking it wit' the other people there. It looked like a normal block party in Chicago. As I continued to scan the crowd, I saw there were about six different groups of niggaz that were ten-deep at a time. They looked like they were overseeing the party, like they were running shit. I made it up in my mind that they were who I was finna chop down.

I took one deep breath, jumped up, and ran to the front of the house, but stayed in the gangway. I got down on one knee and flipped that AR-15 off safety, put my eye in the scope, and watched how the group zoomed into my lens. I smiled and pulled the trigger. *Boom! Boom! Boom! Boom! Boom! Boom! Boom! Boom! Boom!*

The gun jerked in my hands, and I watched the niggaz fall backward with big holes in their chests. Blood spurted into the air, and then they started to run while screaming ensued from the crowd.

I kept on chopping, picking their group apart. *Boom! Boom! Boom! Boom! Boom! Boom! Boom!* More bodies fell. My heart beat faster. More blood spilled. My assault rifle felt hot in my hands. I could see the smoke coming from it, the smell of gunpowder heavy in the air.

Boom! Boom! Boom! Boom! Boom! Boom! Boom! I didn't know where the shooting was coming from, but it sounded like the same kind of rifle I was shooting, so I knew it had to be one of the crew.

It seemed like people were running everywhere, screaming loudly. I turned around and saw people were running through the gangway I was just perched on, a few women holding their children's hands. I started running out of the yard and down the alley toward the garage that had my duffel bag in it.

Boom! Boom! Boom! Boom! Boom! Boom! "Argh! Shit! Help me!" *Boom! Boom! Boom!* Somebody hollered off in the distance.

There were so many people everywhere that I was starting to panic from being seen. They were falling all on the ground, trying to get away with their lives intact. I booked it to the garage, found my duffle bag, and loaded my assault rifle back up, then put it over my shoulder and ran full speed back toward my truck while police sirens screamed in the far off distance.

When I got back to my truck, E was already in the back of it, lying on the floor. He scared the shit out of me at first, but once I saw it was him I calmed down, started it up, and pulled away from the curb, jumping right on to the expressway by the White Sox stadium.

Twenty minutes later we were in Tez's basement, and I was feeling sick because the news was reporting over twenty people had been shot, and eighteen were fatal. They weren't naming the victims or their genders, but I couldn't believe the number.

Tez popped a bottle of Moet. "Now, that's what the fuck I'm talking about. That's how you handle bitness, my nigga! Like them east coast niggaz be saying, word is bond!" He shook up wit' Wayne and they hugged each other.

I thought these niggaz was out of their minds, and E gave me a look that said he agreed. I wanted to get up out of there and go somewhere so I could clear my head. I felt like I needed to be around Madison and Kenosha for a minute, but Tez had other plans.

"Now that we busted that move, I think it's time we start to talk about how we finna take over these projects. How we finna go at J-Rock an' 'em?"

Wayne pulled an already-rolled blunt out of his inside coat pocket and lit it, inhaling a cloud of smoke before blowing it back out. "I say you let me just walk up to dude's bitch ass and blow his head off. Why the fuck should we play around wit' these niggaz?"

E shook his head. "That nigga super plugged. You ain't just finna walk up to the dude and do shit. Trust me, it ain't that sweet. You put a bullet in him, we finna go to war wit' the whole south side and most of the BOs in the city."

Wayne pursed his lips. "Fuck them niggaz. If that's how it gotta be, then that's just what it is."

I frowned. "Nall, we trying to get money first and foremost. Ain't no way we can be beefing wit' them niggaz and still get paid. We gotta come better than that."

Tez took his gloves off and sat them on his chair, then took the blunt when Wayne handed it to him. "What you propose, then, Racine? Because I'm wit' li'l homie right here. I say walk up to that nigga and blow his shit all over the pavement, then the rest of the crew hit they ass up with these choppahs. We gotta let muthafuckas know it ain't sweet, that way other crews don't try us. You already know how Chicago is. Niggaz always looking to take over the next nigga's shit by force, especially if they weak and ain't on shit. We body that nigga J-Rock and go to war wit' them Murda Mafia BO niggas and win, the city gon' bow down to our feet. That's the way the game goes."

As much as I wanted to go for that shit he was kicking, it just wasn't making no sense to me. I didn't think we could get into a war wit' J-Rock an' 'em and make money at the same time. On top of that, we still had Rayjon to worry about. There wasn't no telling when that nigga was gon' resurface, and from what Averie was saying, he was gon' come back hard. We had to be prepared for that, and in order to be prepared, our chips had to be in order.

"Look, I say we drop them niggaz off two and three at a time. They can't be no more than fifty deep, so I say instead of running up on J-Rock and knocking his head off, let's just kill up his niggaz and dump they bodies in Julian Lewis' district. That way we'll be killing two birds wit' one stone. In the meantime, I say we have a sit-down wit' that nigga and make it seem like we gon' be paying him dues to hustle out of the Taylors when all along our play is to hit him from the inside out. Then, when he weak enough, we cut that nigga head off and take over the Taylors for good."

All three of them were looking at me like I was God or something. I could tell they were amazed.

Tez was the first to speak. "That's my boy! My muthafuckin' nigga, cuz!" He got up and hugged me. "Yo, we gon' do shit the way he talking about doing it because it make more sense."

Wayne shrugged his shoulders. "Long as I get to kill up them niggaz, I don't give a fuck. What's good wit' them whips you promised, though?"

E laughed. "I'm riding wit' y'all, so whatever the move is, just let me know for sho'. I could use a nice whip, though."

I smiled. "Y'all getting ten stacks apiece and a whip. It's time we start to look more like family."

Chapter 9

It wasn't that hard to get J-Rock to have a sit-down wit' us. All we had to tell him was we had our own supply of heroin, and we were willing to pay him ten percent off every thousand we made. That was a hunnit dollars. He was wit' it and sent word through E saying he wanted us to have a sit-down so we could set everything in stone. So, two days after the block party shoot-out, me and Tez met up wit' J-Rock and a couple of his niggaz at Harold's Chicken on 73rd. Me and Tez got there first and waited ten minutes for him to show up.

Tez opened the box of chicken he had bought and started to drench it wit' Tabasco sauce. I couldn't believe he could eat at a time like this when that nigga J-Rock could have been luring us to this spot, so he could knock our noodles out. Over the last two months prior to our meeting there had been at least three people killed in front of this restaurant, so it wasn't like it couldn't happen.

He sucked his fingers and flipped his three breasts over, drenching them wit' the sauce. "I hope this nigga take his time. I'm hungry as hell. Fuck, I ain't ate shit all day." He frowned and put some of the Tabasco sauce on his fries.

At first, I wasn't that hungry, but after I got to watching him hook his food up, my stomach started to growl. All the sudden I wanted to get up and order me something.

Tez tore the skin from one of the breasts and stuffed it in his mouth with his eyes closed, chewing happily. I felt like we was finna get in a fight because as soon as he closed his eyes, I grabbed one of them breasts out of his box and bit into it, scooting away from the table a li'l bit. Man, that shit was good and hot – so hot I almost dropped it – but I kept my composure and held it steady while I took another bite.

The crunching must've been kinda loud because he opened his eyes real quick, looked at the piece of chicken I was holding, then back into his box, and just started laughing and nodding his head. "A'ight, I see what you on." He kept on laughing, then pushed his fries closer to me. "I knew yo' ass had to be hungry. We ain't barely been eating shit over the last few days. That grind is real."

I forked up a few fries and stuffed them into my mouth just as that fool J-Rock came through the door wit' eight niggaz behind him. All of them had their hats broke to the right wit' blue rags around their necks. J-Rock had a mug on his face, with a small scar on his forehead. He was a light-skinned nigga, about my height, and about twenty pounds heavier. Before he came to the back where me and Tez was at, he stopped at the counter and, I assumed, ordered some food. Five minutes later he strolled to the back just as I was wiping my hands on a moist towelette.

Tez stood up, and his face matched the mug on J-Rock's face. "What's good, nigga? Long time, no see," he said, extending his hand.

J-Rock looked him up and down and balled his fist. "I don't be shaking hands and shit, homie. I'll give you dap, though, then let's talk about this money." They dapped, and I could tell Tez ain't even wanna do that after what that fool had said.

He extended his fist to me and I dapped. "What's good, nigga? Have a seat."

J-Rock's niggaz snatched up two more tables and put them together, along wit' the chairs from them. "Close this muthafucka down, Sam, until I'm done conducting my bitness back here. I don't want nobody else coming through them doors until I say so. Tell me you understand that," he hollered.

A dark-skinned, balding man came from around the counter with a manager's tag on, nodding his head. "I got you, J-Rock, that ain't no problem. Please, we just don't want no trouble in here today. We can't afford no more murders. The city already talking about shutting us down."

"Hey! I don't wanna hear all that shit. Just shut them fuckin' doors and bring me and my homies our chicken before they be drawing chalk around yo' body!" J-Rock hollered, and I noted the man damn near broke his neck locking the doors.

I could tell I didn't like this nigga already. I didn't like bullies, never had, and the way he was carrying hisself, I could tell he was used to being a bully. When he took his black skullcap off, I saw that he was a bald nigga.

"A'ight, now to you li'l niggaz. Let's talk money and dope. Y'all agreeing to hit my mob wit' a hunnit off every gee y'all make. That's cool, that's ten percent, but there is also a fee for hustling out of the Taylors."

I couldn't help curling the right side of my upper lip. "Oh yeah? And what's that fee?" I asked, looking into his eyes. I was trying to detect any signs of bitch in him, yet all I saw was ice. A nigga who probably didn't have a soul.

"That's a gee a week from both of y'all, so one apiece. I run the Taylors and everything up in them. If I'm gon' allow for you niggaz to impede my turf, then that's what the bill gon' be. Period. Y'all got a problem wit' that?" he asked, looking from me to Tez.

Now I was having visions of popping this bitch-nigga in his face a few times and splashing his niggaz. I ain't like this stud, and I was having a hard time keeping my feelings in check. The worst for me was being humble to a nigga I didn't like. My temper was blazing, and I think it was all because of how he was coming at us like we were some hoez or somethin', and I ain't talking females. I'm talking as if we were soft and wasn't about that hammer life.

Tez nodded. "That's cool, my nigga. Long as we got an understandin', then we ready to get a move on."

"Yeah," I said trying to stick to the script. "We gon' need some security, too. How many niggaz you got that run under you that we can depend on to have our backs because we work under you?" I asked, trying to see how deep this nigga's mob really was.

"At least sixty, and all my niggaz head-bustas, so y'all ain't gotta worry about shit. Long as you pay me what you owe, you can do yo' thing," he said, wiping his mouth wit' his hand.

Sam and two of his workers came over with trays full of chicken and set them down in front of J-Rock, then his niggaz. They all started to eat, and I couldn't help watching all of them niggaz closely.

"Y'all do what you gotta do, and who knows? I might even let you join my mob. You know, I'm finna take over the whole south side, and in a minute niggaz ain't gon' have no choice but to join me or get they ass bodied. Bitchez, too. It's Murda Mafia or nothin'."

All his niggaz got to nodding they heads and smiling just like a bunch of followers. I had been in Chicago my whole life, and I had never been able to bow down and follow behind no nigga. Tez was my cousin, and everything we did was side-by-side. I was my own man, and I could never see myself submitting to another dude. Fuck that. Even playing the role like we were was real hard for me.

Tez laughed. "I say we see how this shit goes first, and if you feel like we worthy to join yo' mob in a few months after you see how we get down, then we'll go from there. I already know you finna take over shit, though. Yo' name ringing in these streets, so that would be an honor, word is bond."

"You damn right it is, and it's best you niggaz get down wit' me or lay down wit' the rest of my opposers." He wiped his nose and grabbed a big piece of chicken, ripping it wit' his teeth, then speaking wit' a mouth full of food. "Y'all have my first few pennies this Friday by one o'clock, and that goes for every Friday. If ever you late, you owe me five hunnit more, no negotiations. I'll send word that you four are free to roam the Taylors. Get money, niggaz. And most importantly, get me minez."

As soon as I got into Tez's truck, I felt like going nuts. I slammed my door as Tez started the truck and pulled away from the curb. "Yo, I ain't never wanted to splatter a nigga's shit the first time I met 'em, but I wanted to kill that cocky-ass nigga. Then I ain't never heard you so humble before to another nigga. That shit was throwing me for a loop."

Tez shook his head. "Cuz, my trigger finger itching like a muthafucka. Just as bad as you wanted to kill that nigga, on my son, I wanted to kill him, too. You know I don't even like them yellow-ass niggaz no way because I can't take 'em serious. The only way I was able to stay cool is because I kept hearing yo' strategy and words of wisdom in my head. We gotta move smart so we can get these chips. It's the only way. But we finna fuck this nigga over, and I'm gon' love every minute of it. Denzell say most of them niggaz don't even stay in the Taylors. I got they real addresses, and we gon' make a few house calls, all in due time. For now, let's just stick to the game plan and flood the hood wit' this dope we got from that nigga Rayjon."

I heard everything he was saying, yet I was still trying to calm down to get ahold of myself. I had never paid no nigga to do nothin' before, and now that we had to pay J-Rock just to hustle out of the projects? Man, I was having a hard time dealing wit' that, even though it was my plan.

I noted Tez was real quiet, and I wondered why. I looked him over for a few seconds and saw he looked sick. "What's good wit' you, cuz?"

He shook his head and swallowed. "I miss Martez, man, and Raven. I can't believe that shit went down the way it did. I never meant to kill my son, man, you know that. Then his mother? Well, I wasn't in my right mind. She reminded me of my mistakes. I couldn't look into her face no more, cuz."

He made a left and got onto the expressway. I was trying to figure out what made him suddenly bring that up. I mean, we were talking about bitness. Nobody had mentioned his past mistakes of him killing his whole family. I was tryin' to get past that because it was fucked up. "What made you bring that up?"

He shrugged his shoulders. "I don't know. I just miss my son, and it been eating at me. I think I need to find me another bitch, so she can have my kid. I need one right away, too, so I can feel better."

I scrunched my face and wanted to say somethin', but no matter what I could have said, it wouldn't have uplifted him one way or the other because I was gon' tell him he was acting and talking like a damn fool. But then we pulled into the woods and up to the spot where he had buried his son and baby mother.

Tez jumped out of the truck, and I followed him. We wound up fifty yards from where he parked with him on his knees, tears streaming down his face. He cleared the leaves from the homemade grave that held his son's body, then rocked back and forth while I stood up, missing Madison. "I'm sorry, son. Daddy miss you, and I wish I never hurt you the way I did. I hope one day you can forgive me."

He cried for a few more minutes, then got up and walked about five feet before kneeling back down. The wind started to blow as the sun set, and I started to feel this real eerie feeling. I didn't know what was coming over me, but I felt creeped out. I looked all around and only saw more and more trees blowing in the wind. I still wanted to get out of there.

"Raven, I'm sorry, baby. I wish things would have been different, but sometimes you just talked way too much. You always got on my nerves, and I couldn't watch you cry over our son no more. That shit ate at me too bad. I'll see you on the other end, and I'll make things up to you if you allow me to. If not, well, then I don't know." He stood up and dusted off his knees.

By the time we got back into his truck, I was ready for him to drop me off. I was missing my daughter, and I wanted to spend some time wit' her.

Tez pulled up in front of my crib and turned to me. "Look, cuz, I'll be here at five in the morning, so we can get on this bitness. I say we hustle until about eleven, then Denzell got a lick for us that should be over a hunnit and fifty thousand, not including the dope. So, it's gon' be a busy day. Get some rest. I'm finna go get some pussy. I feel like some rough-ass sex." He smiled weakly.

I gave my cousin a half-hug, then jogged up the steps to my crib. I didn't even get a chance to open the door before Kenosha opened it and jumped into my arms. I picked her all the way up and she wrapped her legs around me. Behind me, I heard Tez blow his horn before pulling away from the curb.

"Daddy, I missed you so much. I hate when you be gon' all day long like that. Then you never answer your phone or return my text messages. Don't you know that be freaking me out?" she said, laying her face into the crux of my neck.

I didn't feel like getting into all of that, so I crashed her back into the wall and started sucking all over her lips loudly while she moaned into my mouth. I held her up by that fat-ass booty, going under her li'l Prada gown she wore around the house. She ain't have no panties on, and her skin felt hot and soft. I massaged that booty, then slid my hand down and between her legs, rubbing that plump pussy before sliding my middle finger inside of her, and sucking on her neck hard.

"Mm, Racine. You always trying to get out of somethin' by freaking me. That shit ain't gon' always work, I hope you know. Mm, shit."

I worked two fingers deep into her box and started running them in and out of her. Her kitty was already slippery. Her juices oozed onto my hand while she bit my neck like she was angry wit' me.

I opened my pants, then reached between us while I held her against the wall. My gun fell down the back of my pants, and I didn't even give a fuck, I just wanted some of that pregnant pussy. I didn't know who was in the house and didn't care. As soon as my dick was free, I slid him into her tight li'l hole and forced her down onto me roughly.

"Uh. Uh. Uh. Uh. Shit, daddy. Uh. Uh. Yes, daddy. Yes. Fuck me. I. I. I. Been missing you. Daddy. Yes!" she moaned as I moved her up and down my dick, feeling her juices drip off my balls and run down my thighs. She wrapped her arms around my neck and sucked my ear before sticking her tongue in it, then she sucked my throat while I squeezed her big booty and fucked her like a savage up against the wall.

When we fell to the floor, I got to long-stroking her hard and fast, digging into that pussy, rolling my back, and trying to get as deep into her as I could. It was so good I felt like cumming wit' each stroke. I couldn't help groaning and biting into my bottom lip.

Kenosha pulled me down to her and we started sucking all over each other's lips while I squeezed her titties and ran my thumbs across her erect nipples. I didn't know we were being watched until I looked up and saw Jill standing in the living room with her hand in her panties, moving back and forth inside of them. All she wore was white boy shorts and a matching tank top. Both nipples were sticking through the material. Seeing her watching us only made my dick harder.

Kenosha waved her over with her forefinger. "Come here, Jill. Eat my pussy while my baby daddy fuck me from the back. Hurry up," Kenosha ordered before sitting up and making my dick fall out of her. She flipped over to her knees and bent over, her pussy hole wide open and leaking. She reached under herself and spread her lips.

I put my dick right back in that hot pussy and got to fucking her hard while Jill stuck her face under us, and I could feel her licking my balls and sucking Kenosha's lips. She way lying on her back and finger-fucking herself hard with her thighs wide open and jiggling.

"Mm! Mm! Yes, bitch! Eat my pussy! Eat my pussy! While. While, uh! Shit! Daddy! I'm cumming. I'm cumming again!" she screamed and bounced back hard on my dick while her body shook.

Jill kept right on eating her, fingering herself the whole time. I watched her pinch her clitoris, then run four fingers in a circular motion. Juices leaked down her ass, and I was fighting the temptation to touch her pussy. It was so fat.

She squeezed her thighs together and rubbed her pussy real hard before opening her legs real wide and screaming "Aw! Shit! Y'all! This shit feel so good!" She humped into her fingers, and I watched them disappear into her again and again, then I came deep into Kenosha.

I didn't know how they had gotten so cool all the sudden, and I didn't ask, nor care, I just felt like we were one step closer to all lying in the bed together.

I learned my daughter and Remy were wit' my mother this night, so I didn't wind up seeing Madison until the next day.

Chapter 10

It was bright and early the next day, and I found myself in the Robert Taylor Home Projects rocking heroin alongside Tez, wit' E and Wayne on security. Although we had just opened for bitness, that door had been getting beat on non-stop. I couldn't believe how the fien's were coming.

The knocking sounded again, and I went and answered the door wit' E standing behind me wit' his pistol out. "What's good?" I asked, looking through the peephole at a sista so skinny she looked like an upside-down exclamation point.

She waved a bundle of money into the peephole, so I opened the door enough to make the chain stretch out. She adjusted her weight from one foot to the other. As soon as I opened the door, I could smell how musty she was.

She licked her lips and scratched her shoulder hard. "Baby, I got three hundred dollars, and I wanna spend it all, long as you give me a good deal. I been up hustling all night to get this money and I needs me a wake-up," she said, smiling and exposing her yellow teeth. Her breath smelled horrible.

I backed up a little bit and scrunched my nose. "Look, I'll give you thirty-four hits for the three hunnit, and the more I see you, the better the deals'll get," I said, not wanting the conversation to carry on any longer.

Her eyes got bucked. "For real? And it's that same stuff everybody been talking about?" she asked, looking like she had hit the lottery. Three more customers came and stood behind her forming a line.

I nodded. "Yeah, it's the same. Now come on, because you holding up the line."

She handed her money through the crack, and I looked over my shoulder at Tez, who had a thick-ass redbone sitting on his lap with no bra on. Her nipples were big and brown. She lived right there in the Taylors, and so did her two friends who were sittin' at the table bagging up dope wit' Wayne. "Give me thirty-four, cuz."

He nodded, counted them out, and handed them to the li'l broad whose name I had not learned yet. She walked over and handed them to me, licking her juicy lips. "Here you go, homie."

I took the dope and watched her thick ass jiggle as she walked back over to Tez and sat on his lap. I shook my head and gave the dope fien' her work before the next one stepped to the door, bouncing on his toes.

"Say, man, I want that same good shit I got earlier. I'm still feeling them effects, and I been wonderin' where y'all been all my life. These niggaz been around here selling some straight bullshit. Sending people to the hospital and everythang. All I wanna do is groove, baby. I ain't asking too much."

This dude smelled worse than the female. Now, I could tolerate a funky woman for the most part, but when it came down to a nigga, I wasn't wit' that shit. "Look, back up from the door and hand me yo' money. It's the same dope, and you ain't never gotta worry about us selling no bullshit out of here. How many hits you want?"

He went into his pocket and pulled out a Ziploc bag full of quarters. "This fifty dolla's right here. I want five of yo' strongest hits. I'm trying to groove like the Isley Brothers," he said, smiling.

I grabbed the bag of quarters and gave him a crazy look. I wasn't about to take that shit, but then I remembered what my pops had always told me about heroin addicts. He said heroin addicts would be quick to kill you if you denied them their drug, especially if they knew you had it. That they were the most dangerous of fien's to play wit'. I kept that in mind and gave the dude six hits. "Look, this dope gon' always be good. And if ever you need a wake-up just to get yo' day started, I'll fuck wit' you. You hear me?"

He went from smiling to making a sad face like he couldn't believe what I was saying to him. "Damn, man, I honor hustlers like you. You get how the game go. I swear, you ain't never gotta worry about no muthafucka trying to kick this do' in. I'ma keep my ear to the street and make sure everybody know you alright." He took his dope and jogged down the hallway.

The next fien' had a big screen smart TV in his hands, and he looked like he was having a hard time carrying it. He was a short, heavyset man wit' so much sweat on his face it looked like his forehead was peeing. He walked up to the door, struggling to maintain the TV. "Say, li'l brotha, I got this TV, and I only want thirty bags for it. It's brand new. I just took the tag off it."

Tez jumped up so fast the redbone chick almost busted her shit. "Jo, snatch that muthafucka up. We need a TV for the trap, and a video game since we gon' be in here all day. So, let that nigga know we gotta have that bitch."

I couldn't see myself sitting in no trap all day long. My nerves were to bad, and I was always fearing the worst. I was a jack-boy at heart. I liked to rob niggaz and get my money nice and fast. All that waiting around for fien's to come give me peanuts was beneath me. Fast money was the only money worth my while.

I looked back through the crack in the door. "Slide that muthafucka through, and we gon' make sure it work before we hand you thirty bags of this sauce." I pulled the door open a little further, making the silver chain on it stretch all the way out.

He slid the TV in to me. "Man, it's good. I wouldn't never try no shit like that. People done got killed around her for less. I love my life."

Soon as the TV slid through, Tez snatched it up and plugged it into the wall, confirming it worked two minutes later. "Jo, it's good. Give him what he want for it." He sat back in his chair, and the thick redbone repositioned herself on his lap while he played wit' her nipples.

I gave the fien' the dope, and he promised to come back later with a new X-Box 360. That got everybody behind me excited except for myself. Having a video game in the trap was only gon' make my anxiety worse because I would be thinking like I was the only one really on point, and anytime we were hustling, or doing some shit we wasn't supposed to be doing, I felt like we needed to be one hunnit percent focused.

I served ten more dope addicts, then sat down on the one couch we had brought to the trap from the li'l redbone's crib upstairs. That muthafucka looked a li'l dirty and had a spring sticking through it closer to the right arm of the chair. I tried my best to keep that in mind because it had already caught me slipping twice.

Tez patted the li'l redbone on her thigh. "Get up and let me see you twerk in my face. I want my cousin to see how project hoez get it in, so he can get a li'l comfortable in this muthafucka," he said, eyeing her body up and down.

She stood up on pigeon toes and popped back on her legs, causing her titties to swing a li'l bit. "I'm saying it ain't even no music playing. What, I'm just supposed to go off a beat in my head or somethin'?" she asked with some glossy, juicy-ass lips.

Tez reached and pulled up her mini-skirt, exposing her fat, yellow ass cheeks. "I'ma put a beat on my phone but bust this muthafucka open. You thick as a muthafucka," he said, scrunching his face and grabbing his phone. He messes wit' it for a brief second, then that Yo Gotti *Rake It Up* instrumental came on.

It was like her body had a mind of its own. As soon as the music started, she put her hands on her hips and popped her ass, making it jiggle along wit' her thighs. Her tongue stuck out of her mouth as she spread her legs a little more and really got to twerking.

My eyes got big as hell as I watched everything move. I was starting to feel like I had a hunger for thick women, because the more she shook that ass, the hornier I got until my dick was sticking straight up along my stomach.

"Yeah, bitch. Get that shit. Look how fat her pussy is," Tez said through clenched teeth and pulled her skirt all the way up until it sat around her waist and stayed there.

She dropped to her knees and got on all fours, put her face into the carpet, and really started to twerk, making that ass shake. She had a big ghetto booty that a real nigga had to appreciate. I most definitely did.

Tez reached and pulled her panties all the way into her ass, causing her pussy to pop out. She moaned and spread her legs so far apart it was like she was hitting the splits. I noticed her pussy lips had completely swallowed the material of the red lace thong.

Tez started to rub her pussy while her nipples appeared to get harder and harder. "Jo, this finna be my baby momma. I can see myself fucking this thick-ass bitch every day for the rest of my life. You like that, Keyonna?" he asked, sliding two fingers into her box.

She closed her eyes and moaned into the carpet before running her tongue across her lips. "Hell yeah. I'm 'bout what you 'bout, li'l daddy." She jerked her ass harder, riding his fingers. Her lips opened around them, and every time he pulled them out of her, I noted they got wetter and wetter.

Tez pulled her up by her hair. "Cuz, I'm finna go hit this pussy. I'll be back in, like, a half hour. Come on, bitch." He yanked her up by her red hair and they disappeared down the hallway before going into the back room.

***

Later that night we found ourselves sitting in front of Denzell while he puffed on a weed-filled Cuban cigar. He offered me one, but I turned him down because I knew Tez had been getting fucked up all day messing around wit' them redbones, so I needed to have my head clear before we handled this bitness Denzell was about to put us up on.

Janine walked past on her way to the kitchen, and I couldn't help but look down at that ass. She looked over her shoulder and we made eye contact before she turned away with a smile on her face.

Denzell passed the blunt to Tez and sat back in his seat, crossin' one leg over the other one. "The marks I want y'all to hit tonight, I want annihilated, dead. Make this kill a statement kill, because these dudes sinned against me and one of my closest allies. When shit got too heavy and the feds stepped in, they chose to take a deal to testify before the grand jury, and I just can't let that happen. That's not how the game goes." He leaned forward and picked up his glass of scotch, twirled the glass around and causing the ice cubes to bump into each other before he put the glass to his lips and sipped out of it.

Tez was making big clouds wit' the weed smoke and inhaling them hard before blowing it back out of his nostrils. He looked like he didn't have a care in the world, and I was wondering if he was listenin' to this nigga or not. "Cuz, you good over there?" I asked, getting a li'l irritated.

He nodded and took another pull from the blunt. "I'm Gucci, my nigga. G'on 'head, Denzell. Tell us how you want these niggaz fucked over."

Denzell smiled and sat is glass back onto the table in front of the couch. "I want them carved up and put down in a bloody fashion. I want this kill to scream that snitching don't get you a better deal, it leaves you worse off."

I was ready to get shit on the road, but I also needed to know how much we was finna get hit for this move. I remembered him sayin' before that wit' every move there would be large sums of money involved. "So, how much we getting paid for this shit? Or what's in the house that's gon' line our pockets?" I asked, wetting my lips wit' my tongue.

"That's a good question, Racine, and I'm glad you brought that up. If you and Tez take care of these dudes the right way, I'll pay you a hundred thousand apiece. But I want them dismembered and dropped in Julian Lewis' district because he's supposed to have been the one that assisted in their deal. I have to embarrass him and make it, so his word means nothing in the world of politics."

Janine and I made eye contact. The kitchen was behind Denzell's back, so he couldn't see her. She smiled at me, then licked her lips before turning around so I could see that fat ass in the tight Eve St. Laurent blue dress she was wearing. I ogled that ass and didn't give a fuck if Denzell peeped me or not. My old teacher was doing somethin' to me.

"Well, Denzell, all you gotta know is this shit finna be handled tonight. By the morning these niggaz'll no longer be a worry of yours. Now, you sure they all staying in this safe house?" Tez asked, taking another hit from his blunt.

Denzell nodded. "Not only am I sure, but I have arranged for the officers that patrol that area to take their break between eleven and twelve midnight. That's the window you have, so work wit' it. And remember that the whole house must die. Make it as messy as you can. Let me know my two hundred grand is being well spent."

Tez leaned his head back on the sofa and blew a big cloud of smoke into the air. "We got you. Just have that cash ready."

I heard everything that was being said, but I was still busy watching Janine give me the phone sign wit' her fingers and mouthing the words that she was going to call me.

Chapter 11

I held the female's shoulders while Tez duct taped her feet to the chair, then taped her hands and body to the chair as well. After I made sure she was secure, I stepped back and looked over the basement. We had found two females in the house, along with two dark-skinned niggaz who looked like brothers. Both were bald with full beards and real muscular. We'd caught they asses sleeping, ironically enough, and one smack of the pistol had caused them niggaz to fall right in line.

It was an easy entrance straight through the garage, which they had left open. I was guessing because they were in witness protection, they had let all their guards down thinking it was sweet. That made shit easier for us, so I wasn't complaining.

I grabbed the bigger of the two dudes up by his neck and sat him in the chair with my pistol to his temple. Tez taped him to the chair just like we had done everybody else, and I was surprised at the little resistance he put up. All he kept on doing was begging us.

"Say, man, I'll pay you anything. Just don't do this shit to my family. My woman ain't got shit to do wit' this, blood. Let her go, and let my brother's girl go, too. We all got kids. Please, man. Name yo' price," he said, shaking like a leaf.

Tez slammed the other dude onto the chair and I taped him up real good. "Nigga, you give me a hunnit gees right now and I'll let all of y'all go, that's my word," he said, taking a step back and pulling out his deer hunting knife.

The dark-skinned dude poked his lip out and started to sweat. I was ready to tape his mouth shut because the noises he was making was getting to me already. I hated when it was time for bitch-niggaz to die. The sounds they made were irritating.

"If I give you that money, what's to say you ain't gon' kill me and everybody else, anyway? I already know how the game go. I'm from the land, too, my nigga," he said, trying to sound hard wit' tears in his eyes.

I pulled out the same kind of knife Tez had, stepped up to that nigga, and sliced him across the face, then stabbed the knife into his thigh and twisted it with all my might. I could feel his muscles shredding and everything.

He hopped up and down in the chair and hollered at the top of his lungs. "Argh! Argh! You can have the money. I swear on my momma, you can have the money."

I pulled the knife out of his thigh, smiling under my mask. "Where it's at, then, nigga? We ain't got no time to be playin' wit' yo' soft ass. Where the fuck the paper at?" I asked, ready to slice his face up no matter what he told me. I hated soft niggaz, and to me that nigga was soft. Not only was he snitching, but he was crying in front of his woman because he was on the receiving end. That shit was weak to me, so I was gon' kill him no matter what.

"Upstairs! In my room. It's all in my mattress. Cut that bitch open on the side and it's in there, homie. Now, let me and my people go. A deal is a deal," he whimpered.

I took the knife and slammed it into his thigh again, leaving it there while he hollered and jerked around in his chair. "Nigga, which one of these females is yo' woman?" I asked.

He nodded his head to the female to his left. "Her, right there. That's my woman. Please let us go," he said, sounding like he was out of breath.

I walked over to her and ripped the tape from her mouth while Tez stood back and watched me in action. She looked like she wanted to scream. "Shorty, whatever you do, don't scream or I'm gon' kill you. Nod your head if you understand me."

She nodded and blinked tears out of her eyes. "Please don't hurt me. I have a little daughter who is only three. She needs me."

I tried to shake what she just said out of my mind. I could not allow myself to bring any form of a weak emotion into this move, but looking at her face, I was finding it so hard not to. A three-year-old child. Damn, that was fucked up. I shook my head hard. "Look, shorty, is he telling the truth? Is his mattress filled wit' money upstairs?"

She nodded. "Yep, it is because he told me if he got indicted, I was supposed to slowly put it into the bank for him. It gotta be at least two hunnit somethin'," she said through tears.

"Okay, so you can show me exactly where it is, right?" I asked, looking down on her.

She nodded. "Yeah, I can do that. And I don't want none of that money. You can have it all. I just want my life, please."

I shrugged my shoulders. "Okay then. Well, since we don't need this snitching-ass nigga no mo',"

I taped her mouth back, turned on my toes, and slashed the knife through the air and into the dude's face, cutting him deep. He hollered into the tape on his mouth, then I grabbed his forehead for leverage and really started to slice him again and again while his blood splattered across my mask and arms. I kept on slicing, then slammed the knife into his throat and ripped too hard to my left, leaving his neck looking like a gaping mouth. His blood gushed out and into his lap, before his chin fell to his chest. I flipped the chair backward and wiped the knife off on his pant leg.

I turned to see Tez stabbing the other dude again and again in the face. He was grunting, and the dude was jumping up from his chair only to receive more and more stabs to the face. Tez ended him by shoving the knife into his chest and turning it, then he kicked his chair over as well.

He walked to the other female and grabbed her by the hair, yanking her head back. She screamed into the tape and kicked her feet. "Cuz, take that bitch upstairs and get that money while I handle her." He exposed more of the woman's throat, then raised his knife and slammed it right into the center of her neck, where her Adam's apple would be if she were a dude. Her legs started shake uncontrollably.

The other female was screaming loudly into her tape. She started to panic so bad she fell over in her chair and kept on screaming loudly. Tez slammed the knife into the other woman's chest like he had did her dude and ended her suffering.

I reached down, ready to grab the chick who had fallen out of her chair when Tez came and bumped me out of the way. "I see you be having a problem killin' these hoez, but not me. A life is a life. It's no mercy. Fuck these bitchez." He yanked her up by the hair and threw her toward the stairs. "Bitch you finna take me to this money or I'ma torture yo' ass and find yo' daughter. I ain't playin', neither. Get yo' ass up them stairs!"

He turned to me. "I'll meet you in the whip, cuz. I got this shit."

That was the last I saw and heard from the girl. Before I left the basement, I looked around at all the damage we had caused. Necks were ripped open and blood was everywhere.

For some reason, I started to miss my daughter.

***

That night we got back to Tez's crib and discovered the niggas was holding a hunnit and seventy-five thousand dollars. We busted that shit down the middle and went our separate ways.

When I got to my crib, the first thing I did was go into Madison's room and climb in the bed wit' her. Remy was asleep on one side, so I entered on the other and scooped my baby girl into my arms, kissing her on the forehead. I could still smell the death coming from myself, and I just needed to hold her. Killing always made me feel some type of way. I mean, it came natural to me, but it was the after-effects that always got the better of me. I knew life was short and my time was coming real soon, and I tried daily to make peace with that fact. When I died, I just wanted to make sure my daughter and her mother was always straight.

Madison slowly opened her eyes and smiled at me. "Is that you, daddy?" she asked through a raspy voice. Her breath smelled like cinnamon.

I kissed her on her dimpled cheek. "Yeah, li'l momma, it's me. I missed you, baby, and I just wanted to hold you." I hugged her tight.

She grunted, then wrapped her arms around my neck. I could tell she was still sleepy. "Daddy, can I go wit' you tomorrow? Because I haven't in a long time, and you're my daddy, so I should."

I kissed her on the forehead and held her close to my chest. "Yeah, baby, we can go anywhere you want to go. Tomorrow will be your day because you're my baby girl. How does that sound?"

She nodded and closed her eyes. "Can Remy come too? Because she don't have a daddy."

I kissed my baby again. "She sure can. We'll let her spend some time wit' us, that way she can know how it feels to have a daddy that loves her."

Madison hugged me tighter as I scooted onto the bed. I fell asleep after I heard her snoring on my chest. My daughter always healed me and brought me down to earth. I knew I was living on borrowed time, but as long as I was there, I was going to make sure she was spoiled.

The next day I got them dressed bright and early in the morning and we hit up Gurney Mills, a large shopping mall located outside of Chicago. I let those girls run in and out of stores getting whatever they wanted, no matter how much. By the time we made it to Toys 'R' Us, I was carrying so many bags I could barely walk straight. I put them in my truck, then took them into Toys 'R' Us and spent damn near five thousand dollars. The entire back of my truck was filled with their things, and I had a bunch more delivered.

After Toys 'R' Us, I took the girls to get their hair done at Top Notch beauty salon. While they sat in their chairs, I touched basis wit' Tez just to make sure everything was running smoothly. After confirming it was, I sat back and chilled until it was time for my girls to be done. From there we went to Barbie's Oasis outside of Chicago, and I let the girls wear themselves out by playing and eating pizza until their bellies hurt.

By the time we made it home, they were fatigued and in a deep sleep. I kissed them both on their foreheads and covered them wit' the blankets after plugging in the little night-light.

"Damn, you're an amazing father. Do you know that?" Jill said, peeking her head into the door of Madison's room.

I slowly backed out of it and closed her door. Jill acted like she wasn't gon' move until I rubbed up against her, so I guess she got her wish when I nudged her a little bit. "I just do what I'm supposed to do. I love my daughter, and I'll do anything for her."

Jill laid her head on my shoulder. "I believe you. I wish more men were like you." She took a deep breath and exhaled. "You know it's about time for me to get my own spot, right? I been looking online for apartments, and I found a few in Zion. I think me, and Remy will be safe there. The rent's cheap, and I don't know anybody out there. It'll be a clean escape. What do you think?" she asked, smiling warmly.

I pulled her li'l thick ass into my arms and hugged her, feeling all that heat coming from her body. She smelled like Suave deodorant, that powder fresh shit. "Wherever you trying to move to, I'll make sure yo' rent paid up for the year. And we gon' get you a whip. I wanna make sure you and Remy are straight for the long haul. So, make sure the place you pick is up to par, and I'll take care of the financial aspect of things. I got you."

She wrapped her arms around my neck and hugged me close. "I know you do, Racine. That's why I love yo' ass so damn much. Ever since you came into my life, I've been happy. You make me feel so secure and safe. I am thankful for you." She stepped onto her tippy toes and kissed my cheek.

Kenosha cleared her throat, causing me to look into the kitchen where she stood wit' her hand on her hip. Both thick thighs were exposed under some tight red boyshorts that were all up in her crease. I looked down and noted her pretty toes were painted. I don't know why I noticed them in that moment, but I did. "Excuse me, but I need to break up this lovey-dovey-ass moment and steal a few minutes wit' my baby father, if that's okay wit' you, Jill?" She rolled her eyes and raised her left eyebrow.

Jill backed out of my embrace and nodded. "I'm sorry, Kenosha, but you already know how Racine is. This nigga so kind it be making me weak. Damn, I'm sick over him. That's why I gotta get out of here before I jump out the attic window or somethin'," she joked, but there was seriousness in her voice.

Kenosha walked over to me and grabbed my hand, looking Jill up and down defensively. "Well, it's best you do that because this nigga right here belongs to me. Don't get shit twisted because he done hit yo' pussy a few times. This is my dick," she said, grabbing my pipe and pulling me by it.

I curled my upper lip at her gangsta while Jill threw her hands into the air. "I know. I already know, girl. That's why I gotta get out of here."

After we got into my room, Kenosha closed the door, and stood in front of me as I sat on the bed. "Why the fuck you go out and buy them li'l girls all that shit? Damn, you spoiling Remy more than you is me. Ain't I the one pregnant wit' our child?" she asked, looking heated.

I already knew that wasn't gon' fly right when Kenosha saw them bags. She didn't even like when I did more for Madison than I did for her at one time. She was my BM, but at the same time I was like a daddy to her. That's what made our relationship so strong. "Baby, that li'l girl needed that, and you already know anything you want, I'll go out and get that shit wit' no hesitation. You are the mother of my children, and I value you wit' my life. You know how I get down, so it ain't no reason for us to even be arguing about this petty shit."

As soon as I said that, I was trying to find somethin' I could come up wit' so I could get out of that room. I ain't feel like going back and forth wit' Kenosha. She was an extremely jealous female, and I understood that, but I also felt like Remy didn't have anybody in her life who could blow some chips on her. Every little girl needed that.

Kenosha took a deep breath and exhaled, shaking her head. "I already know all of that, and it's really not about you spending money on me. I just don't like you spoiling this bitch's kid because it's gon' make her fall in love wit' you just like she doing. I already gotta compete wit' all them other hoez in the streets. I don't need to be competing wit' a bitch that live under my roof." She sucked her teeth loudly. "Damn, don't you understand the way to a woman's heart is through her children, if she got them? You be forcing these hoez to fall in love wit' yo' ass. It don't even be they fault." She sat down on the bed beside me and laid her head on my shoulder.

I guess I understood what she was getting at for the most part, but I didn't see things that way. All I saw was a little girl who didn't have nothin', whose mother was trying to do the best for her with the little she did have. I felt as a man it was my duty to step in and help out. But instead of saying all of that, I simply put my arm around Kenosha and kissed her on the cheek. "I love you, baby, and you ain't never gotta compete wit' nobody because don't nobody measure up to you. You always gon' be first and foremost. I promise you that."

She closed her eyes and smiled when I kissed her on the forehead. "Well, I hope so, because my self esteem is getting lower and lower the more pregnant I become. I don't know what this second child is going to do to my body, but whatever it does, you better love me extra hard. I'm not playin', either." She turned her head and looked up at me wit' her eyes searching.

Now, I know she just needed a little validation, but her comment irritated me a little bit. "Kenosha, when have I ever not loved your body? Or when have I ever made you feel like I loved you less because of your body?"

She shook her head slowly. "You've always made me feel good about my body, I'm not saying you haven't. I just know I'm probably going to look a little different, and females are already always all over you. I'm just a little concerned that one day one of them will snatch you all the way from me, then I'll have nothin'. I'm getting to the point I want you all for myself, anyway." She exhaled loudly. "When do you think we'll be able to be on some one-on-one shit for the rest of our lives? When we hit twenty-five? Thirty? What?" She turned all the way, so she could look into my face.

I really didn't know how to answer her question in that moment because I didn't want to lie to her. There was no doubt in my mind I was goin' to marry Kenosha one day, but I didn't know if I saw it being soon because I still had a real bad lust-bug inside of me. Whenever I saw a nice-looking female wit' a big-ass booty, I wanted to know what that pussy felt like and how she handled that big muthafucka. It was somethin' in me I didn't understand, and I wasn't mature enough to completely shut down those urges.

I wanted to explain all of that to her, but I didn't feel like I could the right way, so I made her straddle me and held her face in my hands, looking her dead in the eyes. "Baby, I love you, and you should know I'm gon' be wit' you for the rest of my life, riding until it kills me. Far as us being together on some one-on-one shit, you already know I ain't ready for that yet, but in time. We just twenty-two, but I'll get there. And when I do, that's when I'ma put that ring on yo' finger. Those streets are crazy right now. When I get down on that knee, I wanna be able to leave the streets completely, and everything that comes along wit' it. I'm gon' wanna be all about our family, that's it."

She leaned forward and kissed me on the lips a little hard before sucking on them and pulling back. "You always kept shit one-hunnit wit' me. That's why I love you so much," she smiled. "Well, I'm ready now because all I see, and need is you, and so will our children. So, Racine, when you're ready, I'ma be there wit' my arms wide open. I promise you that." She closed her eyes and laid her head on my chest.

I rubbed her back and hugged her firmer. "It's gon' be you, Kenosha. You're my baby, and you gon' be my wife. That's on our children."

Chapter 12

Me and Tez hustled for two weeks straight before that nigga J-Rock came beating on the door to the trap one Sunday morning like he was the fuckin' police, and that's when things took a turn for the worse. I was sitting at the table, just putting the last bag of heroin into the Ziploc when this clown got to beating on the door so loud it made me, Tez, E, and Wayne pull our pistols out.

I ran to the side of the door wit' my .45 against my shoulder. "Man, who the fuck is it beating on the do' like that?" I hollered, ready to start busting through the door. There was no way I was finna let no police take me down to Cook County Jail. Me and that nigga Tez had too many enemies in that mutha-fucka. We'd probably get killed on day one.

There was a loud-ass kick to the door. *Whoom!* "Nigga, this J- Rock. Open this muthafucking do' before I shoot this bitch in and hurry up!" he hollered and seemed like he had an attitude.

I frowned and looked at Tez, and he was already giving me the same look, like this nigga had lost his mind. I paused for a brief second then took the chain and two-by-four off the door, opening it. J-Rock walked right into the apartment and bumped me out of the way. I almost raised my gun and blew the back of his head off. I hadn't never let no nigga bump me before and get away wit' it. I was feeling like a soft-ass bitch by letting him do it, and I almost didn't.

Tez bit into his bottom lip, and I could tell he was just as heated. "Damn, nigga, watch where the fuck you going. You bumped my cousin hard as hell," he said, mugging the shit out of J-Rock.

Some fat nigga from J-Rock's crew stepped into his face, and I pushed the shit out of him so hard he fell over a chair and wound up on his back. "Fuck-nigga, this ain't that," I said, looking down on him.

J-Rock and the other three dudes in his crew upped their handguns and looked like they were about to shoot me when Tez, me, Wayne, and E aimed our guns right back at them. I didn't know what them niggaz was thinking, but everybody was finna die in that bitch, and in that moment I didn't even care. I hated them bitch-niggaz.

Tez stepped up to J-Rock wit' his gun in his face. "Fuck you niggaz on? Y'all come up here on that dumb shit?" he asked wit' his finger on the trigger.

Behind him the fat nigga started to get up. I noted the side of his head was bleeding. I didn't see where he had hit it at, but I was guessing the corner of the table.

J-Rock scrunched his face and mugged Tez with anger. "Nigga, you betta get that gun out my face or we gon' have some serious problems. All of us," he said through clenched teeth.

Wayne pumped his automatic shotgun and curled his upper lip. "Tez, let me know what's happening. On everything, I ain't bowing down to these niggaz. This our trap," he said with his finger on the trigger, ready to squeeze.

"Bruh, what's good? Why you niggaz come over here beating on the do' and shit? We in here hustling. Y'all fucking up our paper," I said, getting more and more annoyed. I could still feel where that nigga had bumped, and it was getting to me.

"I just want my cash. Y'all been hustling for two weeks plus, and I ain't seen shit yet. Up my dough, or we can turn this muthafucka into the Fourth of July."

I was tired of holding my pistol at these niggaz without busting. I felt like shit was looking weak as hell. It was either we was finna blow some shit up or talk like civilized men. "Look, we got yo' paper, J-Rock. We was just waiting for you to come get this shit." I lowered my gun because them niggaz ain't look like they was gon' bust. I went into my pocket and pulled out a knot that was J-Rock's cut. I held it up, so he could see it. "This you right here, homie."

He lowered his gun and smiled, then Tez and everybody else lowered theirs. Except for Wayne. He kept his shotgun aimed at J-Rock.

"Now, that's what I'm talking about," J-Rock said as I handed him the bundle of cash in all hunnits. He thumbed through the bills and laughed out loud. "This all I come fo'. I shouldn't have to beat on this muthafuckin' do' for what belongs to me. Next time y'all hit my phone or it's gon' be trouble." He looked from me to Tez, then to E, and lastly Wayne before his eyes got bucked. "You holding that shotgun like you gon' pull that trigger or somethin', nigga. Why the fuck everybody else done put they shit down and you still got yours up? Huh?" he asked, walking toward Wayne.

Wayne rolled his head around on his neck before scrunching his face. "Nigga, I'm on security until you niggaz get the fuck out this trap. You know how this shit go."

I saw the look in Wayne's eye, and I knew he was gon' pull that trigger. That was gon' make us be caught in the middle of a big-ass war wit' J-Rock and his allies. We couldn't afford that at the moment, so I had to diffuse shit before it blew up.

I walked in front of J-Rock. "Look, from now on we'll make sure we get you that paper on time. That's my bad because I'm responsible for that shit, but I got you from now on. Until then, why don't you niggaz let us get back to hustling so we can make this paper?" I looked to my left and could see fien's lined up in the hallway. I had forgotten to close the door 'cause that nigga J-Rock bumping me threw me off.

J-Rock mugged Wayne for a long time, then nodded his head. "Yeah, a'ight then. I'ma let you niggaz get back to y'all bitness, that way I can get my paper at the end of this week. I guess I'll see y'all around. Come on, BDs."

I watched them walk out of the door. The fat nigga turned around and mugged the shit out of me wit' hatred in his eyes. He smiled, then turned around and followed behind J-Rock and his crew.

As soon as they walked down the hallway, I told the fien's I would be right wit' them in a minute, then closed the door. "Bruh, we killing them niggaz. I hope y'all know that. Ain't no way we finna let them hit us first," I said, already knowing J-Rock an' 'em was finna be on some bullshit. It was written across all their faces.

"We should've let li'l homie blow that nigga head off his shoulders, because he think shit sweet.

I'm tempted to go gun them niggaz down in the hallway right now. Ain't no sense of playin' wit' them."

Wayne jogged toward the door wit' the shotgun in his hand. "You ain't said shit. I'll go knock that nigga's noodles out right now. Just give me the word," he said, taking the chain back off the door.

I waved him off. "Nall, we gon' be smarter than that. Let us holla at Denzell to find out where that nigga lay his head, because he don't live in the Taylors. Once we get that info, then we'll body his ass and get on somethin' new. What y'all think?"

Tez nodded and pulled at the hairs on his chin. "Sound like a plan to me."

E stuck his hand in the White Castle bag and pulled out a burger, taking the wrapper from it. He shrugged his shoulders. "I'm wit' it. Long as I get to splatter somethin', I'm down." He closed his eyes and bit into the burger, chewing and shaking his head.

"Long as I get to torture that nigga J-Rock, I'm down for whatever," Wayne said, setting the shotgun up against the wall.

I knew we had to get rid of J-Rock fast or that fool was gon' come for us. We had committed a cardinal sin by the rules of the slums of Chicago. You were never, and I mean never, supposed to up a gun on somebody and not kill them. The rules said if you did, then it was their right to kill you on sight the next time y'all ran across each other. So, at that moment it was kill or be killed.

***

The next day while Kenosha was sleeping, I decided to roll Jill out to Zion, Illinois where she had a house showing with a realtor. We really didn't say much to each other on the ride out there, and I was cool wit' that because it was kinda early in the morning and I had not gotten much sleep the night before. I had J-Rock and his niggaz on my mind. I wanted to kill them so bad, but I knew we had to be smart about it because he had plenty niggaz that rolled wit' him all throughout the city. Had we just knocked his head off and word got out, we would have had drama wit' niggaz we didn't even know.

While Jill had her meeting, I locked all the doors of the truck and took some time to doze off. I didn't wake up for a half hour, when I heard her knocking on my driver's side window loudly. I jumped and went to reach for my .45 until I saw her face, then I popped the locks.

She sat in the passenger seat and closed the door. "Damn, you must be tired, huh?" She smiled sympathetically.

I ran my hand over my face. "I'm good, shorty. What happened in there?" I started the ignition as the sun beamed through the clouds, heating me up.

"It went well. The rent is going to be nine hundred a month, three hundred for utilities, so a total of twelve hundred." She looked out of the window, then down at her lap as if she were sick.

"Look, I'm just gon' give you fifteen gees even. That way you can pay up yo' rent and utilities for the month, and that li'l left over you can keep. Now come on, because we still gotta go and get you a whip so you and Remy can be straight." I stepped on the gas and got onto the expressway.

Jill was quiet for a long time, just staring at me as if somethin' was wrong. I looked over at her and noticed her eyes were real glossy like she was about to cry, and I didn't know what was going on. I crinkled my forehead. "Jill, what's good?"

She blinked tears and started crying with her face in her hands, shaking her head from side to side. "I can't take this, Racine. I love you so fuckin' much, and I need to be wit' you. I don't know how I've made it this far in life without you, but now that I know what it feels like to have you, I never want to be without you again. Even Remy loves you as much as I do." She cried harder. "No man has ever reached for me the way you do, and I don't even know why you care so much because I don't have anything to offer you. I barely have anything to offer my daughter. So why do you care so freaking much? Huh?" she asked, turning to me.

I switched lanes on the expressway and sped down the highway with the El Train on the side of me along its tracks. "Look, Jill, I ain't got the answer you need to hear from me. I guess real men do real things. You deserve a break, sista, and I'm able to give you that. I care about you and Remy, and I just gotta do my part. Y'all are females, and no females should have to figure things out on their own in this cold-ass world. I do what I'm supposed to do, and as long as I'm out here trapping, I got you."

She shook her head, looking me over. "I guess I'll never understand you. I'm just gon' chalk it up that God is working through you. But I will say this:

for as long as I am alive, I will submit to you and do any- and everything you ask of me because I truly love you. I'll never overstep my bounds because I know who you ultimately belong to, but in my heart and in my mind, I am your woman, too."

I ain't have no response for what she'd just said, so I chose to remain silent like I was in court or somethin'. In my eyes she wasn't my woman at all, and she didn't owe me a damn thing. I was just doing what I was supposed to. How many niggaz would have allowed a female to go through the things Jill did without offering to help her, especially if they had the means? I was a street nigga, but I still understood I had to protect those that needed protecting, and Jill and her daughter Remy needed exactly that.

I let the SZA record play through my speakers, laid back a li'l bit in my seat, and got off the expressway. "You said you want me to swoop by your mother's crib, so we can pick up Remy, right?" I asked, slowing my speed and turning along with the road until I came to a complete halt at the stoplights on Cottage Grove.

She nodded her head. "Yeah, my mother wanted to spend some time wit' her, but now she gotta go to work, so she called me while I was in there meeting wit' the realtor and said I needed to pick her up."

"A'ight, that's cool."

She sat back and rode in silence until I pulled up at her mother's house, located on 51st and Aberdeen. When we got there, Jill hopped out of the car and closed the door. "I'll be right back. She should already have her ready for me," she said and jogged up the steps. She had on some tight-ass Jordache jeans that made her ass sit up right. I couldn't help shaking my head. I figured I was gon' hit that shit before the day was over wit'. I had to. Them jeans was doing somethin' to me.

While she was in the house, I switched the music over to Yo Gotti and sat back in my seat, nodding my head. The sun was shining bright as hell, giving me a headache. I flipped down my visor and looked at the clock on my phone. It was just after one in the afternoon. I checked my rear-view mirrors, then looked around at the hood I was in. I knew they called it Moe Town, and I ain't have no bitnesss being over there. Me and Tez had clapped at a few of the niggaz from the area, and I was just praying Jill hurried her ass up before they started to come out and post up on the block like they usually did in this area.

Just as the thought crossed my mind, I saw the front door to Jill's mother's house open and little Remy appear wearin' a pink Prada coat I had bought her when I took her and Madison shopping. Then Jill appeared holding her hand. I saw her give her mother a hug before the door closed, and they made their way down the steps. I popped the locks on my door, preparing for them. That was another rule in Chicago: you never was supposed to sit in your whip wit' the doors unlocked. That was a fast way to get yo' ass jacked.

As Jill made it to the bottom of the stairs, somethin' told me to look to my right, and I did. What I saw made me hold my breath and reach under the seat for my pistol at the same time.

Three masked men ran from the side of Jill's mother's house with guns out. They ran in front of

Jill, and I saw the taller one pump his shotgun and fire. *Boom*! His first shot knocked little Remy's head right off her shoulders. She flew backward and wound up on the pavement wit' blood spewing out of her neck. Her face looked like it had exploded.

"Ah! No!" Jill screamed and knelt to help Remy, not paying any attention to the shooters.

One of the other masked men opened fire on her, busting back-to-back. *Boom! Boom! Boom! Boom!* His bullets slamming into her midsection before she fell backward, bleeding profusely.

I lowered my passenger's window and let my .45 bark. *Boom! Boom! Boom! Boom! Boom! Boom!*

A few of the bullets hit the nigga that was holding the shotgun. He fell to his knees, then landed on his chest before another one of the masked men got to shooting at me using a Tech .9 *Bop-bop-bop! Bop-bop-bop! Bop-bop-bop!* His bullets shattered my driver's side window and hit the body of my truck before he and the other one who had shot up Jill took off running through the back of Jill's mother's house.

I pushed open my door and ran to Jill's side. She lay on her back with her eyes wide open, struggling to talk. Her chest heaved up and down. No words came out, just blood.

I scooped her up and sat her in my passenger's seat, then ran around and jumped into my truck, speeding away from the curb on my way to the Christ Hospital located in Hyde Park.

Chapter 13

I turned the bottle of Hennessy up and swallowed it in big gulps. I was trying to numb the pain from the loss of Remy. I felt like shit because, had I been on point, I would have been able to prevent her and Jill from being blind-sided. I didn't know what to do wit' myself.

Tez slammed the hunnit-round magazine into the AR-15 and shook his head. "Nigga, I didn't even know you gave a fuck about shorty like that. I can tell you illing 'cause I ain't never seen you go at a bottle like you doing."

I took another long swallow and felt the liquor warm my belly, causing me to be under the influence of its painless antidote. I wiped my mouth wit' the back of my hand and lit the blunt that was sitting in the ashtray, inhaling the thick cloud of smoke hard.

Tez sat down across from me and grabbed the bottle of Hennessy off the table. "She gon' make it, though?" he asked before turning it up.

It was three in the morning, damn near thirteen hours after everything had taken place, and I was still feeling just as sick. I blew the smoke out and nodded my head. "Her mother said the doctors say she gon' be straight. I got her to the hospital just in time. But it's still fucked up for her daughter, though. This the second one she lost. I can't imagine how she gon' be once she come out of that drug-induced coma they put her in. That would be hard on any mother." I took another strong pull from the blunt and lowered my head as Tez passed me back the bottle of liquor.

"Cuz, at least you was able to save her. You can't be so hard on yo'self. You ain't no muthafuckin' Superman. You know how this game go, and you know how them niggaz in Moe Town get down. Shorty ain't have no bitness being over there. It was money on her head ever since she admitted to knowing who it was that kilt her oldest daughter. So, it ain't yo' fault, Racine. It's hers."

I hopped up off the couch and stood in front of him wit' my face balled up. "Nigga, it is my fault. Had I been on point, I would have smoked them niggaz. I just slipped, and because I did, I got two females hit up." I felt sick on the stomach.

Tez stood up and looked me over closely, then lowered his head and hugged me. "You just got a good heart, cuz, and it ain't for me to knock you fo' that. You'll be okay, and we'll get through this shit because it's all a part of the game. The best way I feel like you can get yourself back mentally is to come wit' me and the homies so we can fuck this nigga J-Rock all the way over."

I sat on the couch, feeling my head spin. "You must've got his info from Denzell?"

Tez picked up another AR-15 and slammed a clip into it loudly. "You already know. I know where this nigga, his bitch, and the kids stay at. I wanna body this nigga and let the li'l homie Wayne do his thang on him. What I didn't know was J-Rock kilt that li'l nigga Wayne's brother back in the day when Wayne first moved up here from Milwaukee. J-Rock don't even know he did it, so it's gon' be real sweet watching the li'l homie torture his ass until his life leave his body."

My head was spinning like crazy. All I could see was Remy's little face and Jill inhaling bullets while I sat in the driver's seat, trying to get to my fo'-nickel. I wish I could have done more for them. That shit was gon' eat at me forever, I felt like. I was hoping Jill remained strong and got better so I could be there for her when she got out. I knew for a fact I was gon' take care of her for as long as I had life in my body because I would never forgive myself for letting them come under fire like that.

Tez smiled and put his hand on my shoulder. "I'm telling you, once you see what we got in store for this nigga J-Rock, you'll feel a lot better."

I nodded. "When y'all trying to make this shit happen?" I asked, taking a seat on his couch. I was missing Madison and Kenosha. I felt like I needed to be in their presence just, so I could know they were okay. I needed to be around them just, so I could feel a little bit better.

Tez grabbed the bottle of Hennessy and turned it up before burping and wiping his mouth. "Don't even trip, cuz. Let me and li'l homie an' 'em get everything situated. When we got the nigga, I'm gon' call you and let you know where to meet me. Until then, why don't you go home and get some sleep. You look like shit."

I had every intention of taking his advice, but when I got home Kenosha and Madison bum-rushed me at the door, wrapping their arms around my waist and stomach. I picked Madison up and put my arm around Kenosha's shoulder, kissing her on the cheek. She smelled like she had just gotten out of the shower.

"I missed you, Daddy, and I was sad because you were gone." Madison said, laying her head on my shoulder. I could feel her heart beat against me, and it made me feel strong. I loved my daughter.

"I missed you, too, baby. Daddy been thinking about you all day long." I said walking to my room. I needed to get somewhere so I could sit down. I was feeling dizzy as hell and like I had over did it.

Kenosha rubbed my back. "Baby, are you okay? Because the last time you called me and told me about what happened, you sounded real sick. Now you're drunk. This isn't like you," she said with concerned eyes.

I sat on my bed, and she sat down next to me while Madison kept her face in the crux of my neck. "I'm good. I just feel like I could have done more. That girl done lost two kids now. I know that's gon' kill her. I could only imagine the pain she's going through."

Kenosha laid her head on my other shoulder. "Well, baby, you gotta move on, because they weren't your responsibility to begin wit'. And in my opinion, you've already did all you could. Just think if I would have let Madison go over to Remy's grandmother's house like I was about to, because her and that little girl were begging me to let her do so. Man, can you even imagine that?"

I swallowed the lump in my throat as that picture played over in my mind's eye. I don't know what I would have done if anything would have happened to my daughter, especially somethin' like that. I took a deep breath and held Madison tighter. "I just thank God it wasn't the case."

Kenosha reached across me and stroked Madison's long, curly hair. "Well, it very well could have been. You been protecting them ever since all of that stuff happened wit' her other daughter. You've done all you can, baby. Trust that. We need your protection, not nobody else," Kenosha said, kissing my cheek.

I hugged up with the both of them until I felt my eyelids get heavy, then I passed out and didn't wake up until I heard my phone buzzing like crazy on my nightstand. I sat up in bed after removing Madison's arm from around my neck, grabbing the phone and reading the face. The call was from Tez, and he was letting me know he was on his way to my crib for bitness.

I jumped up and got into the shower, trying to wash away the darkness of the day before. Even though I didn't want to admit it, I was missing Jill and worried about her well-being. I'd taken heed of everything Kenosha had said, but there was still a part of me that felt like I could have done more. More than once it crossed my mind about going to see her, but then I thought about all the police and detectives that were all around her, trying to find out what took place with her and Remy's case. I knew I was on fire, and there was no telling if they were already lookin' for me for a variety of murders me and Tez had committed.

So, even though I felt sick and wanted to drop in on her, I just couldn't. It was way too risky.

As soon as I stepped out of the shower and got myself together, Tez was blowing his horn outside. I slipped on my Timms and jumped into his passenger's seat after kissing Kenosha and Madison. I loved my li'l family, and I couldn't wait to get back to them that night, especially Madison. After what had taken place wit' Remy, I felt like I needed to cherish my daughter more and spend more time wit' her, because life was indeed short.

The inside of Tez's truck smelled like a strong batch of loud. I noted E was in the back eating a juicy-ass gyro. As I was taking my seat, he was just biting into it, holding it wit' two hands and wit' his eyes closed.

"What's good, cuz? You a'ight?" Tez asked, pulling away from the curb and puffing on a fat-ass blunt that was rolled in Cuban paper. That let me know off the bat Tez had been in tune wit' Denzell most recently.

I nodded. "I'm good. I had to shower to get all that negative energy off me, but I'm cool now. So, what we on."

I heard that nigga E burp. That made me turn around in my seat and mug his heavyset-ass. He sucked up his pop through a straw, then burped again. When he noticed I was mugging his ass, he frowned, then laughed. "Oh, my bad, big homie. I ain't ate shit all day, so I'm enjoying this muthafucka right here. What's good, though?" he asked, taking another big bite. I damn near wanted to ask him for some, as good as he was making it look.

Tez looked into his rearview mirror. "Nigga, cover yo' nasty-ass mouth. Don't nobody wanna be smelling yo' gyro-ass breath. Damn, my nigga," he said, frowning.

I shook my head and turned around in my seat. "I'm good, Tez. Now, y'all niggaz tell me what we on for the night, 'cause on some real shit, I wanna go hug up wit' my daughter and pregnant BM," I said, being honest.

Tez shook his head and turned onto Halsted Street before hopping on the expressway. "Nall, you ain't finna do that. We got that nigga J-Rock and a few of his main niggaz right where we want they ass. Denzell set some shit up, and he can only hold them for so long."

I scrunched my face. "What you talking about, Tez? How is he holding them?" I asked, confused as hell. I didn't know what the fuck my cousin was talking about, and I really wasn't in the mood to figure it out.

Tez switched lanes on the expressway and passed a big-ass white truck, then switched to the lane the truck was in and got in front of it. "Right now, he at J-Rock's crib, and they having a meeting with J-Rock and some of his advisors. The move is he want us to body J-Rock and the niggaz he got wit' him. For this move he gon' hit us wit' two hunnit bands, but it's just one catch." Tez lowered his voice as he said the last part.

I could hear that nigga E in the back smacking like a muthafucka, and it was throwing me off. "E, please! Damn! Don't you know how to eat without doing all that extra shit?" I hollered and felt myself getting heated. I hated when people smacked while they ate. That was a pet peeve of mine.

"Damn, my bad, big homie. I'm done wit' this shit now, anyway." I could hear him balling everything up and putting it into a bag he had wit' him.

"Look, cuz, I know you on edge because of everything that happened, but I need you to have yo' head right now because shit finna get real. Now, the catch is after we body J-Rock and his niggaz, we gotta take J-Rock and at least one of the other niggaz's bodies and lay them in Julian Lewis' house. And that's after we kill him, too. Denzell say if we do all of this shit, he can guarantee that over the next few months we'll be making three hunnit gees a day out of the Taylors, and he'll help us move our cartel southward through Vulture City."

I ran my hand over my face and tried to wrap my head around what Tez was saying to me. I didn't have a problem wit' killing up J-Rock and his dudes because I didn't like them niggaz anyway, plus I was sure in time they were going to clap at me and Tez because we pulled guns on them while in the projects. But to kill an alderman was something else. That meant the police level was about to be turned all the way up, and I didn't know if I was ready for that.

I exhaled loudly. "Tez, when we supposed to do all of this shit, huh?"

He smiled, evil-like. "Time is money, nigga, so we gon' handle this shit tonight."

Chapter 14

I cocked back my .45 with the extended clip and crouched down on the side of J-Rock's house as Tez did the same thing beside me. I watched him pull out his cell phone and send a text.

"A'ight, now all I'm waiting on is for Denzell to open this bathroom window right here. Once he do that, we finna climb through this bitch and get at them niggaz. It's four of them all together, and that fool family here, too. So, we gotta be careful and make sure we don't miss his bitch, 'cause she could call the police. They conducting bitness in the backroom. Denzell said when we first kick the do' in, he gon' be seated to the left of the door, and J-Rock is to the left of him. One of his niggaz is to his left, and the other two standing up on security, so we can't play no games."

I wasn't planning on doing that, anyway. I wanted to go in there and body these niggaz and get this shit over wit'. I was feeling a li'l apprehensive about us killing all these people and leaving Denzell to have so much leverage on us. It was just somethin' about him I didn't trust. I mean, for one he was setting up some niggaz he'd been dirty hustling wit' for a few years. Who could tell me in a year or, so he wouldn't do the same to us? To me, he seemed like a snake. "A'ight, that sound good, cuz."

E cocked his Mossberg pump. "I'm ready to blow some niggaz's heads off. Wayne already in position scoping out Julian Lewis' crib, so after we handle this bitness, we can bounce straight over there and handle him," he said, adjusting his mask on his face.

Tez's phone rang. He read the face, then looked up at the window just as the wind blew full-force and kicked dirt up. It was pitch black outside. All the streetlights on J-Rock's block had been broken out, which played to our advantage.

The window opened, and Denzell stuck his head out. "I'm ready. Now, y'all don't fuck up and hit me. We got a deal, right?" he asked, looking concerned.

Tez waved him off. "Nigga, you good. We'll be in there in less than two minutes, go take yo' seat and stay as far left as you possibly can."

Denzell nodded, swallowed, and disappeared back into the house. I could hear the toilet flushing.

"Look, if y'all saying he got a woman and children in there, somebody gotta go in and get them before we even get at them niggaz, because you know she gon' scream. So, how we gon' do that?" I asked, already picking apart our spur-of-the-moment plan to do somethin' this severe. I felt like shit like this took at least a few days' planning. We was stupid for trying to hit these niggaz up in one day.

Tez pulled his mask all the way down. "A'ight, when we get in there, I'ma snatch up the bitch and kids. Then we'll kick they door in and handle them. I mean, what other way is there?"

E shrugged his shoulders. "Sound good to me. Let's go," he said, standing up.

I pulled him back down. "Look, that shit sound stupid. This what we gon' do. When we get in there, me and E gon' hold them niggaz at gunpoint until you find his woman and kids, Tez. Once you locate them, you bring them to where we are, and then we'll handle them niggaz. Unless we see her first, and then we'll just snatch her up and go from there. How many kids is it, anyway?" I said, already dreading the fact more children might have to be killed.

"He got two twin boys that are six," E said.

"A'ight. Look, Tez, don't kill them li'l boys unless you have too. Shorty, neither. We just knock off J-Rock and his niggaz and get up out of there wit' they bodies. Understood?"

Tez laughed. "Nigga, yeah right. You know I'm killing they ass. I don't give a fuck about they lives. I ain't like you." He stood up and climbed through the first-floor bathroom window. After I gathered myself a minute later, I climbed in behind him, and E followed me.

As soon as my heavy breathing stopped, I could hear SZA on the radio somewhere off in the distance, and I smelled the aroma of chicken. My stomach growled, but I took that to mean J-Rock's woman was in the kitchen cooking, which should have made things easy for Tez.

It was right then I made up my mind I was gon' snatch up her and her kids because I didn't want Tez killing them for no reason. "Look, cuz, I'll handle the family. You and E handle them niggaz. Let me snatch her up first, and then I'll join y'all."

Tez nodded and whispered, "A'ight, cuz, but smoke that bitch if she get to acting stupid. I don't know what it is wit' you and killing hoez, but you gotta get over that shit because it's a part of the game. So, handle yo' bitness."

"I'll buck that bitch if you want me to," E said, getting down on one knee with the Mossberg up against his shoulder. "Killing is killing to me. I love this shit."

I shook my head and waved him off, twisting the doorknob until it opened the door that led into a short hallway. I stepped out of the bathroom and entered the hallway, creeping down it on my tippy-toes. I passed one door that sounded like a bunch of men was in there laughing. I figured it was J-Rock and the rest of his crew, along wit' Denzell. They sounded like they were having a good time.

I continued on my way until I got to the end of the hall, looked to my left, and saw light coming from the kitchen along wit' a dark-skinned female who grooved while she seasoned her chicken and laid it into the frying skillet. I imagined she was Kenosha right away, about to be gunned down for things she probably knew nothin' about, and it made me feel sick. I took a deep breath to calm myself, and then mentally flipped a switch in my head that allowed me to do what I knew I had to.

I crouched down, then as fast as I could, ran into the kitchen and wrapped my big hand around her mouth and snatched her up while she screamed into it.

"Argh! Argh! Argh!" She tried to get away from me by wigglin' her hips and butting her head backward over and over.

I held her as tight as I could and put my lips to her ear. "Look, shorty, if you don't chill I'ma have to kill you, and I don't wanna do that. I know you got kids. So, calm the fuck down and tell me where yo' li'l ones at," I said, shaking because my adrenalin was rushing. "I'ma take my hand off yo' mouth a li'l bit so you can answer me." I did.

I could feel her knees buckle. "Why do you want my kids? Please, don't hurt them," she whimpered.

I shook my head. "I don't want to hurt yo' kids, but yo' man finna die. I just wanna make sure you and yo' kids don't get in the way and get hurt yourselves. Do you understand me? So, you must tell me where they are, or they will get killed, too."

She blinked tears. "Oh my god, this is really happening. Please don't kill us. We don't know anything about what's going on wit' my man. It's not our fault. Please, don't hold us accountable."

I heard the door slam inward down the hall. That let me know Tez and E was on bitness. I had to speed up or the situation was gon' get away from me. "Where are your kids?"

"They're in my room, asleep on the bed. I just put them down. Please, don't hurt us." Snot ran out of her nose and trailed down her lip until it went into her mouth. She swallowed.

I grabbed her more aggressively. "Show me where they at. Hurry up!"

We speed-walked until we were outside of her bedroom with me behind her. Once there, she opened the door and pointed at the two little boys who were knocked out and lying across her bed. Inside of the room was a big screen television that played a Spiderman movie.

I removed my hand from her mouth as I heard a bunch of ruckus down the hallway. It sounded like tables were being flipped over along wit' a bunch of other stuff. "Please, don't hurt us. I swear I won't say anything. All I care about is my babies."

She cried, and I felt sorry for her. I nodded, still imagining she was Kenosha. "A'ight, look. Just turn around, and I promise I won't kill you or them. You got my word on that."

Tears sailed down her cheeks and dripped off her chin. "I just want to raise my kids. We don't have nothin' to do wit' this, so please don't kill us. I'll turn around like you asked." She closed her eyes and turned around, lowering her head.

As much as I knew I was supposed to, I just couldn't, and I wasn't about to kill her. I took the .45 from my waist, turned it upside down, and slammed the handle into the back of her head about five inches up from her neck, knocking her out cold. Then I straddled her sons one-by-one and knocked them out the same way before laying them on the floor next to their mother and rolling them under the bed.

After I closed her bedroom door behind me, I jogged down the hall and got to the room J-Rock and everybody else was in just in time to see E stuffing the barrel of his Mossberg down J-Rock's throat while Tez pistol-whipped one of the men so bad his scalp was wide open with blood sputtering out of it in globs. He kicked his feet while Tez beat him again and again until he stopped moving. Tez stood up and stomped him in the chest. "Bitch-ass nigga."

The other two men who had come wit' J-Rock lay on their stomachs wit' their hands above their heads. Tez had both of their pistols right by his foot.

Denzell stood up and adjusted his tie. "This is what you get, J-Rock, when you decide you are bigger than the game. Let this be a lesson to you. Finish this negro," he said, waving him off dismissively. E looked to Tez, and Tez nodded.

Boom! J-Rock's head exploded on his neck and splashed against the wall behind where he was sitting. His brain matter flew over all of us. It looked like bloody chitterlings and smelled just as bad.

I knelt down and put the .45 to the back of the first dude's head who was on the floor and pulled the trigger. *Boom*! His head jumped, then opened, spilling out its contents all over the carpet and making a big mess. I felt nothing. No remorse. I just wanted to get this shit over wit', seeing as we still had to body Julian Lewis.

The other dude tried to get up, and Tez grabbed him by the throat, slammed him into the wall, and pulled the trigger, knocking a hole in his forehead. *Boom*! Then he dropped him to the carpet while he leaked from his tomato.

Denzell wiped his hands on his coat. "Well done, gentlemen. Very well done, if I might say so myself. Now, what about his woman?" he asked, looking us over.

Tez put his gun on his waist. "Cuz already handled that, right, cuz?" he asked, looking at me.

I nodded. "Yeah, let's get the fuck out of here. Come on, niggaz," I said, opening the back door and getting ready to run out of the house when I noticed nobody followed me.

I got all the way to the backyard when Denzell ran out and jogged past me. I'll see you li'l dudes later." He ran toward the alley.

I got ready to hit the alley, too. "Where bruh an' 'em at?" I hollered.

He stopped in his tracks and turned around. "Oh, he found Tasha. He's taking care of her." Then he took off running.

I sprinted back into the house, down the hallway, and got outside of her bedroom door when I heard the shots go off. *Boom! Boom! Boom!* I could see the bright light of the gun flashing every time the trigger was pulled, illuminating the hallway.

Tez and E nearly knocked me over running out of the room. "Come on, man, let's get the fuck out of here!" Tez said, running down the hallway along wit' E.

I had every intention of following them, but first I just had to see what he had done. I knew it had to be Tez because E had a Masburg, and the shots I had heard was from a handgun. I opened the door all the way and walked into the room as I heard sirens off in the distance, screaming like somebody in pain. When I got all the way into the room, I saw Tez had laid the mother and her two kids on their backs in the room and shot them all straight through the forehead, execution-style.

I felt sick to my stomach. He had left their eyes wide open. I took a second to close all three sets, running out of the room just as I heard brakes being slammed on in front of the house, along with seeing the flashing lights of the cops.

I took off running out the back door and down the alley. It didn't take much before I caught up to Tez and E's heavyset ass. We took alley after alley until we located Tez's truck, which was parked inside of an abandoned garage.

Chapter 15

By the time we got to Julian Lewis' crib, Wayne had gone berserk. I knew shit was fucked up when Tez got a text from Wayne telling us to enter through the patio door. I found that odd because I thought, just like with the J-Rock murder, we were going to have to creep through a window of some sort. So, when Wayne pulled open the patio door and stood before us with blood all over his black sweater and mask, I just knew something wasn't right.

His chest heaved up and down before he stepped to the side. "Y'all come on in, man. That fool in there, lying on the floor beside the couch. He had a bunch of white people come through unannounced, and I panicked. I think I overdid some shit," he said and pulled out a cigarette.

Tez stepped past him, followed by E and me. I looked him up and down and noted how the blood was splattered all over his clothes, and he made it seem like it didn't matter. I mean, I didn't know if it did or not, but judging by his demeanor, it was almost like it was the most natural thing in the world to be walking around wit' somebody else's blood on you.

I stepped further into the house and my eyes got bucked as hell, because Wayne had gone completely nuts. The first thing I saw was a white man and a white woman laid up against the wall with their throats cut wide open. Blood poured out of their necks and dripped down to their chests, where it left a big burgundy stain on their clothes. The white man was dressed in an all-black-and-white suit, and the white lady had a matching black-and-white dress.

Their eyes were wide open like the sista and her two kids. The smell of death was in the air. It smelled like spoiled milk.

I walked past the dead white couple and shook my head. Looking across the living room, there was a black dude who looked to be about eighteen or nineteen. He was slumped to the side on the all-white leather sofa with four big holes in his chest that were leaking blood. It looked like somebody had left the faucet running. The blood slowly poured out of him, onto the sofa, and finally the carpet, where it turned the white carpet copper-red.

In the middle of the floor was an older black sista. Half of her face was blown off, and there were small brain fragments all over her dress and the carpet. Under her was a pool of blood. I noted the other half of her face was sprayed against the couch.

I could hear moaning and groaning and saw Julian Lewis was behind the couch with a gag in his mouth. Both of his hands were duct taped behind him, along wit' his ankles. He had tears all over his cheeks, and I could see he had pissed himself because the front of his crotch was drenched.

Tez looked around and held his arms out at his sides. "What the fuck you do, Wayne? We was just supposed to kill dude's bitch-ass. This four extra bodies, right here."

Wayne took a pull from his cigarette. "They was here. You already know I wasn't finna kill the dude and leave they asses alive. That ain't how I get down, so it is what it is. Had you told me I could have just killed the dude, you wouldn't even have known about these other muthafuckas," he said, walking over to Julian Lewis and stomping him in the face.

The man's head cocked backward. He groaned in pain, then turned over onto his side, bleeding from the nose.

I shook my head. "Look, bruh, we was supposed to bring a few of them bodies of J-Rock an' 'em and drop them in dude's area, but that shit don't make sense now because he finna die. I don't know what the fuck going on, but let's just handle this bitness and get the fuck out of here. We don't know how powerful these people are that bruh bodied. For all we know, twelve could be on they way over here right now." I pulled out my .45 and walked toward Julian Lewis. I didn't give a fuck what they were getting ready to do, but I was getting up out of there. None of it felt right. I was also starting to conclude I was gon' kill Denzell. He had too much dirt on us now, and he could use it at any time he wanted, too. That fool had to go. Any idiot could see that.

"Yeah, let's get up out of here, cuz. This bitch gotta be hot. Body that nigga and let's go," Tez said, already heading for the patio door.

I nodded and got ready to blow Julian Lewis' face in when Wayne bumped me out of the way and smoked 'im. *Boom! Boom! Boom! Boom! Boom! Boom!* His body jumped into the air as each bullet slammed into him again and again. Wayne looked down on him for a few moments, then put his pistol on his hip.

"Let's go, bruh!"

Minutes later, I was in Tez's truck while E and Wayne drove off in the stolen whip Wayne had gotten before he handled Julian Lewis and his people. I had so much shit on my mind I could barely think straight.

Tez took his mask off and stuffed it between his legs. "Fuck! That nigga Wayne out of his mind, cuz. We was just supposed to hit dude's ass, not all them other people. I don't know what Denzell finna say about this shit. What if that white dude was some kind of connect of his? You think dude gon' be happy about that?" he asked as it started to rain outside. The rain splashed against his windshield before sliding down it.

The wind picked up and I could barely see out of my window. I was missing Madison and Kenosha. "Dude gotta go, cuz. Point-blank. We'd be stupid as hell to let this man have all this info on us and live to tell whoever he wanted too. I don't know what you gon' do about it, but I'm killing dude's bitch-ass as soon as I get the opportunity. We in way too deep. This shit ain't sitting right wit' me at all," I said, feeling butterflies in my stomach.

Tez was quiet for a long time. He drove through the streets of Chicago wit' Twista spitting out of the speakers of his system. "Cuz, what about the Taylors? You mean to tell me we did all of that shit to J-Rock an' 'em for nothin'? Do you understand how much drama we finna possibly face behind all of that?" he asked, looking at me for the first time.

I scrunched my face and pulled my mask off. "Nigga, I ain't said shit about us relinquishing the Taylors. We still gotta get money, and we definitely ain't did all of that shit for nothin'. What I'm saying is dude gotta go. We don't need him to handle bitness. Chicago dirty as hell. They ain't gon' do nothin' but appoint another corrupt politician, and we'll do bitness wit' whoever that is. Right now, Denzell living on borrowed time."

Tez slowed his speed, then stopped completely when the red light popped on Halsted. "Cuz, I know you smart as hell, so if you feeling like he gotta go, then that's law. We'll fuck him over first thing in the morning, no matter what. That way it's before all that other shit hit the news and he catch wind. He won't have no breath in his lungs to snitch about nothin'."

I was feeling like we should have never laid in the bed wit' the dude to begin wit' because I never did trust him.

The light flipped green and Tez didn't notice. He was too busy fucking wit' the bass and treble levels of the music.

"Cuz, pull off. The light green."

He lifted his head up, eyed the road ahead, and slowly eased his foot off the brake pedal, causing the truck to move forward, crossing the intersection.

My stomach flipped ten times in a row because I felt like something wasn't right. Somethin' told me to look to my left, and when I did, I almost fainted. An all-black Cadillac Escalade that looked oddly familiar sped through the red light and came at us full-speed.

"Tez! Hit the brakes, nigga!"

He slammed on the brakes. *Er-uh!*

Vroom! Whoom! Tish!

The truck slammed into us and caused our whip to do a complete three-sixty. The back of my head slammed against the seat, then I shot forward just as my airbag deployed.

Tez hollered and wound up lying halfway on top of me. I heard the doors of a car or truck slam close, and then lots of footsteps on the ground before the gunfire erupted.

Boom! Boom! Boom! Boom! Boom! Boom! Boom! Boom! The windows to the truck shattered and glass flew into my face and along my neck. More shots erupted. *Boom! Boom! Boom! Boom! Boom! Boom!* Something crashed into our truck again, slamming into it so hard it flipped onto its side.

"Argh! Shit, cuz! I'm hit! I'm hit!" Tez groaned at the top of his lungs.

We were both on our sides, him on top of me. It was the first time I noticed how much my cousin weighed. I felt like he was crushing me. I got to feeling sorry for myself, figuring it was how I was going to go out. I had always imagined my death being much different.

Tez's blood leaked into my eye as he struggled to sit up. "Argh! I got at least three bullets in me. I feel them shits."

Boom! Boom! Boom! Boom! Boom! Boom!

Flick! There was a bright light, and then the truck was on fire. Now I was really panicking.

Er-uh! I could hear the wheels of the tires spinning as the truck drove away from the scene.

"Tez, get up, nigga. We gotta get the fuck out of here! Now, cuz!" I hollered, using all my might to force him upward and off me. The truck was getting hot, and I couldn't breathe the way I needed to.

Tez hollered and slowly climbed into the back seat of the truck, took his gun, and shot out the back window. *Boom! Tish!* Then I watched him climb out of it with me right behind him.

As we made it out of the truck, the rain started to come down even harder. Lightning flashed across the sky. Tez lay in the middle of the street, unmoving. I knelt beside him as cars flew past us on the busy street. I lay my head on his chest and panicked when I couldn't hear anything. "Shit!" I got to administering CPR, even though I didn't know for sure what I was really doing. "Come on, Tez! Come on, cuz! Please, don't die on me, bruh! I need you in this world, nigga! Come on, man!" I pumped his chest harder and faster with tears rolling down my cheeks.

Chicago was so fucked up that it had to be about fifty cars that passed us, before one stopped to help, and I couldn't believe my eyes when I saw the face of Ellie all dressed up in her police uniform. She jumped out of an all-white Chevy Lumina, ran over to us, and knelt beside me. Before she even noticed it was me, she tried to help.

"Step aside, sir, I got this. You're doing it all wrong." She nudged me aside and got to doing CPR the right way. After every thirty or so chest compressions, she'd pinch Tez's nose and blow into his mouth twice, then she'd go back to pumping on his chest.

I looked around, and cars continued to fly by. I was starting to worry we were about to be hit or somethin'. "Look, Ellie, we need to get him in your car and to the hospital. He ain't gon' make it out here if we don't hurry," I said, looking around nervously.

T.J. Edwards

She popped her head up and looked me over closely after she heard me call her name before tilting it sideways. "Racine? Oh my god, is that you? I thought you were going to call me, you liar." She punched me on the shoulder, then shook her head hard. "Fuck, now is not the time. Let's go!"

I helped her get him into the backseat of her car, slammed the doors, then we sped away toward Loretta Hospital. Tez lay on the backseat, quiet and still as a board. I didn't know if he was alive or dead, and it was freaking me out. "Is he gon' be okay, El-lie? Tell me somethin', please."

She shook her head with her eyes wide open. "I don't know. I couldn't hear a heartbeat, and that scared me. I'm just praying we can make it to the hospital in time. What happened to him?" she asked, stepping on the gas.

"We was robbed, and the niggaz shot up our whip. That's my cousin, and I need him, man. I don't know how I'd make it in these streets without my right hand."

My brain was racing so fast I couldn't even put together all that had happened. I didn't know who it was that had ambushed us because it could have been so many different people. I was lost and sick, and I needed Tez to be alright. I didn't mind warring wit' the whole of Chicago just as long as I had him beside me. I mean, I know my cousin wasn't perfect and that fool was a little off, but he was all I had in those slums.

"Fuck, Racine. There are going to be so many officers that are going to want to know what happened

164

to him. Are you clean? Like, will you be able to talk to them without being arrested? Be honest wit' me."

"Hell nall, I ain't clean. And he ain't, neither. So, I don't know how you gon' work yo' magic, but I'll pay you to keep this shit anonymous. Just name yo' price," I said, already fearing the worst for Tez. I was feeling like even if he pulled through, he would wake up in handcuffs unless Ellie handled bitness and made it so he didn't.

She drove in silence, mumbling to herself. "Hey, to be honest wit' you, things are a little tight for me right now. My car note is coming up, and so is my rent. You take care of those two things for me and I'll keep this between us. You have my word. But also, in addition to that, I want to get to know you better. You know, on better terms." She flew through a red light and turned the corner, flying into the Loretta Hospital parking lot.

"I got you. Take care of this for me and you will never have to worry about them bills again for as long as I'm alive. That's my word to you."

She jumped out of the car and I helped her load Tez into a wheelchair, then I jumped into a yellow gypsy cab that had a skinny female driver with piercings in her nose.

Chapter 16

I didn't get more than three blocks away from the hospital, when my phone vibrated in my pocket. I was still imagining the holes that were in Tez's shoulder and chest. I was praying he was okay. I didn't know what I was going to do, or who me, E, and Wayne were going to hunt down and kill after we bodied Denzell, because that was still happening. It had to.

I looked at the face of my phone and saw my mother's picture pop up. "Momma, what's the matter? Are you okay?" I asked, automatically assuming the worst.

"Baby. Baby, I need you to get to my house right away. If you don't, he gon' kill me. Please, Racine. Mommy needs you," she said, and it sounded like she was being choked at the same time.

"Momma! I'm on my way. Just hang on. Please," I said, feeling my heart go into my mouth. I didn't even care who it was causing my mother harm. I just wanted to get to her and save her. If I got there and had to trade my life in for hers, I would do it in a heartbeat because she was my world.

I gave the cab driver her address and told her to step on it just as the rain started to come down so hard the driver had to slow down. I imagine she couldn't see a thing, because I couldn't, and it was freaking me out. I thought about somebody hurting my mother, and I knew I couldn't stomach it. She was a pure woman, good natured and God-fearing. I had always known her to be kind to others, and she'd give the shirt off her own back. I knew she was paying the price for my sins, and I would never be able to live wit' myself if I allowed that to happen.

Thirty minutes later, the cab pulled up in front of my mother's house and I paid her before jumping out and running up the stairs two at a time while the rain pelted against my back and drenched my clothes. I got to the door, pulled out my .45, and was prepared to start beating on it wit' all of my might when the door opened, and I was met with the smiling face of Rayjon.

I jumped back just a little bit and felt my heart leap into my mouth. I thought about raising the gun and blowing his brains out, but something told me that would have been the wrong move.

He curled his upper lip and pointed his .44 Desert Eagle at my forehead. "Nigga, get your ass in here and see what I got in store for yo' back-stabbing ass. Let's go!" He yanked me inside by my shirt and flung me against the wall.

Once again, I had visions of raising my gun and blowing his head off, but my common sense wouldn't allow me to do it. I knew he had to have something up his sleeve. I had worked under him for a little while, and I knew how he got down.

He walked up to me, snatched my gun out of my hand, and backhanded me across the face so hard I spit blood across the wall. "Bitch-ass nigga. I helped you and yo' dirty-ass cousin get money, and this how you repay me?"

He picked my head up and spit into my face with a thick-ass, yellow loogie. It went halfway into my eye and halfway onto my cheek before oozing down and dripping from my chin. I rushed him, and he upped both guns and pressed them to my forehead, mine and his.

"Fuck-nigga, I dare you."

I paused in my tracks and took a deep breath, and that's when I looked over his shoulder and the light to my mother's living room flicked on, showing me two of his goons had her tied to a chair with shotguns to her head. My eyes got super big, and I felt sick.

"Look, Rayjon, I'm here now. You can let my mother go, because this ain't got nothin' to do wit' her. This is between us men."

He let me get those words out before he punched me so hard he knocked me out. When I awoke, I was tied to a chair by a rope and duct tape. I struggled against my bonds and tried to break loose, but it was of no use. I was stuck.

My mother sat across from me, butt-naked and duct taped to a chair identical to mine. Rayjon circled around her, groping her, runnin' his finger along her cheek. "This a fine older woman right here. I gotta give you that, Racine. Yo' momma look good." He licked his lips, then kissed her on the cheek and squeezed her left breast so hard I saw her face wince in pain. She hollered into her duct tape. "You know, I usually don't even get down on hoez like this, but ever since you and that bitch Averie crossed me, I hate all niggaz and all hoez."

He leaned his head down and sucked her breast into his mouth. I could hear the sucking noise, and it made me sick on the stomach. My mother closed her eyes as tears fell down her cheeks.

When Rayjon picked his head up, he'd left her breast wet and shiny from his spit. Her nipple looked distended. I struggled against my bonds. I wanted to kill the dude's bitch-ass. I wanted to torture him until he stopped breathing.

I could not take it anymore, but then it got worst. He opened his fatigue jacket and pulled out a long, ridged knife and rubbed the side of it across her face. Not cutting, only threatening her. My mother tensed up and looked like she was about to become hysterical.

"You know what, Racine? I watched my mother and father die in cold blood, and I ain't never been the same. A man never knows how much he can take until he watches somebody close to him die in cold blood."

He yanked her head backward by pulling her hair. I heard her yelp, and then his face scrunched into a frown. He ran his finger along the thick vein on the side of her neck, licked his lips, and smiled at me. "Out of all the niggaz I had runnin' under me, I trusted you, Racine. I trusted you 'cause I ain't see that snake shit in you. I thought you was one of them stand-up-type niggaz, but money'll bring out the true nature of any man." He went into his pockets and pulled out a pair of black latex gloves, putting them on his hands one at a time.

"Rayjon, get off this coward stuff and let's me and you do this like men. You can let my mother go. She ain't got nothin' to do wit' none of this," I said, fearing the worst. I knew how Rayjon got down, and I had a feeling he was about to do the unthinkable to my mother. That was gon' kill me. I didn't know if I was strong enough to handle that.

He smiled at me and smirked at his homies who were holding my shoulders. "Nigga, once you took my money and made my bitch turn on me, everybody became fair game, especially yo' mother. You see, I gotta hit you where it hurts. That nigga Tez next. But then again, he done kilt up his own family, so I still gotta figure his situation out." He took a step back and snapped his fingers. "Make sure y'all hold that nigga good and pay close attention."

I saw both niggaz holding me down nod their heads. I tried to jump out of my seat, but these dudes had me held down good. I felt sick on my stomach, and at the same time like a bitch because I couldn't save my mother.

Rayjon pulled the tape back from her mouth just a little bit. I knew he did it just so I could hear her screams of pain more clearly. It was a tactic most stick-up men used to get their victims to turn, or whatever they were robbing them for. It was nothin' like hearin' somebody you love scream and groan in pain. It would often weaken the strongest of killas.

"Rayjon, dawg, I got all of yo' money and then some. You ain't gotta do this to my mother, man. Let her go. She a female. This between us niggaz," I said in my last attempt at getting him to see things my way.

He laughed. "Yeah, a'ight nigga. Just wait on it." He raised the knife over his head, then slammed it into my mother's shoulder with a bloody plunge. I watched the whole blade disappear into her flesh, before the blood started to spurt all around it.

She tried to jump up from the chair. "Argh! Argh! Help me, son! Please! Help me!"

Rayjon continued to hold her down with a menacing look on his face. I tried to leap from my chair with all my might, but the beefy goon behind me wrapped his arm around my neck and squeezed, cutting off my airway before slamming me back to the chair.

Blood spilled out of my mother's shoulder around the blade. Rayjon pulled it out and yanked her head backward again, exposing her throat. "Nigga, what would make you cross me? Wasn't I fair to you bitch-niggaz? Didn't I keep y'all eating every single day?" He slammed the knife back into her shoulder and drug the knife downward, causing a huge gash to appear. Then he pulled the knife back up and drug it down again while she screamed at the top of her lungs and tears fell down my cheeks.

"This shit gon' cost yo' moms an arm and a leg, my nigga. I'm gon' show you who really run this cartel. This shit in my DNA. My father started this shit, and this how we get down." He ripped the tape off that kept her arm held tight to the chair, then he grabbed her wrist and started to turn her arm counterclockwise over and over roughly. I could hear her bones popping as she screamed, and her eyes rolled into the back of her head.

I tried my best to jump from my chair again, so much so that me and the niggaz holding me down fell to the floor with them huffing and puffing to contain me. I was crying so hard I couldn't breathe.

Rayjon cut the rest of the tape holding her to the chair and threw her to the floor. He had my mother lying on her side with her arm twisted awkwardly. He stomped her in the ribs, slammed the knife back into her shoulder, and started sawing into her with his face scrunched up. I could see her flesh tearing while blood spilled out of her rapidly. He put his Timms onto her ribs and pulled with all his might. Her shoulder joint snapped. He stabbed the knife into the open gash, wiggled if, and pulled once again with sweat coming down his forehead. "Ah-uh!" One last tug and her arm separated from her shoulder while Rayjon continued to saw away at it, cutting apart the last bit of skin that held everything together. Large squirts of blood shot up from my mother's shoulder and sprayed against the wall. She shook on the floor with her eyes rolled into the back of her head. Saliva poured out of her mouth and ran down each cheek.

I felt like the worst son in the world. I felt like it was all my fault. I cried harder and wanted to beg Rayjon to save my mother's life, but I knew he had already made his mind up, so it would have been pointless. I wished at that moment he would have taken my life, so I would not have to watch him take hers. My mother was my everything. She was all I had in life outside of Kenosha and Madison.

Rayjon threw her arm by me on the floor. I noted it still had her wedding ring on its finger. Blood oozed out of the socket where the arm was supposed to be attached to her shoulder.

Rayjon started laughing. "This some shit my father would do." He shrugged his shoulders. "They always said the apple don't fall too far from the tree."

He reached down and grabbed my mother by the hair, dragging her across the floor. "Racine, where all my money at, nigga? I wanna know where every penny at right now, or I'm finna torture this thick-ass bitch some more. Fuck her, she ain't my momma," he said through clenched teeth.

I could barely breathe. I felt the goons picking me up and throwing me back into the chair roughly. I looked up at Rayjon with extreme hatred in my heart for him. I knew for a fact one day I was gon' cut that nigga up into little bitty pieces and eat his bitch-ass. "Nigga, I told you I'll give you every penny. I got all of yo' paper in my safe. You can have that shit, just leave my mother alone. That's all I'm asking you, bruh."

He straddled her and looked back at me, smiling. "Nah, it ain't just about the money wit' me, kid. I know I can get that shit back any day. I'm on some revenge shit right now, and I need you to watch how big homie get down, because next I'm fuckin' over yo' daughter and yo' baby momma. We gon' have some fun today, Racine, word is bond." He raised the knife and slammed it into my mother's left hip, then pulled downward, opening her flesh. Blood poured out of her in a river, then spilled to the floor. He leaned on the knife, wiggled it, and drove it further into her hip.

By this time all my mother could do was scream weakly. Blood poured out of her nose while he sawed away at her before taking her ankle and using it to twist her left leg repeatedly while he lay on the floor wit' her.

I struggled against my bonds. "Momma! I'm sorry, momma! I swear to God, I'm sorry, and I love you so much. I would have never let this happen to you had they not caught me off guard. I'm sorry. I swear I am," I said wit' snot running down my nose and tears streaming down my cheeks. I just made my peace with the circumstances because I knew he was going to kill her. I had to honor that part of the game. I was now thinking about Kenosha and Madison. I knew I wasn't strong enough to watch him do to them what he was doing to my mother. I was gon' beg for this nigga to put a bullet in my head first.

Rayjon pulled on my mother's leg before stomping directly on the spot where her thigh connected to her hip. Her bone snapped loudly, then he started to saw away her flesh like he'd did with her arm. That nigga was that sick, I couldn't believe it.

She could barely let out a sound as her left leg came off her body with blood shooting everywhere. Rayjon took her leg and stood up, holding it in the air before resting it on his shoulder as if it were a base-ball bat or something. "How you feeling, Racine? You feel like that bitch-nigga that you is, or should I go on torturing yo' mother?" He laughed and slung her leg to the floor.

I refused to give this nigga a response. I was ready to kill his bitch-ass, and as soon as I got my opportunity, I knew I was going to.

He walked up on me and squatted down, looking me in the face. "You just didn't know who you was fuckin' wit', did you? You thought I was gon' let you and yo' punk-ass cousin rip me off along wit' my bitch, and I wasn't gon' do shit. You kilt my li'l nig-gaz, and y'all running around this muthafucka like it's sweet. Nigga, this ain't that."

He sucked his teeth real loudly, then turned his back on me before straddling my mother, who was lying on her back with her chest heaving up and down. He grabbed her by the throat. "Look, lady, it's time for lights out. I got other muthafuckas to kill tonight." He raised the knife, then brought it down into her chest once, then twice. Then he was stabbing her again and again with. It sounded like he was punching her in the chest, it was so loud. "You. See. This. Shit. Racine? You. Did. This. Shit. Nigga. You! You! You! You! And that bitch! That! Punk! Ass! Bitch! Averie! Averie! Ah!" He started stabbing like crazy.

I closed my eyes and imagined the faces of Kenosha and Madison. He was saying they would be next. I could only imagine what he had in store for them. I felt like throwing up. I had to find a way to protect my babies. I was their last line of defense. I couldn't allow them to wind up like my mother. I had to figure shit out.

"That. Bitch! That. Bitch! That. Bitch!" Rayjon continued to holler as he stabbed my mother again and again.

Every time I heard the knife go into her body, I felt like dying. It was the worst pain I had ever been through, and I knew I would never be the same again.

Suddenly everything was quiet, then I felt him grab my jaw in his hand. My mother's blood wet my face from him transferring it to me.

He squeezed my mouth. "Nigga, now let's go get you punk-ass daughter and yo' bitch. We really finna have some fun." He muffed me, then stood back. "I want y'all to take that bitch and bury her somewhere and hit my phone when it's done."

Chapter 17

I sat in the backseat of the truck with two shot-guns pointed at my temples. There was one on each side of me, and the niggaz had them pressed so hard to my temples blood leaked down the side of my face and dripped from my chin. The only thing I could think about was my daughter and Kenosha. I didn't know what Rayjon had in store, but I had to find a way to save them.

I cleared my throat. "Rayjon. Look, homie, you done kilt my moms, dawg. Why don't you just get yo' money back, and all yo' dope, then kill me and leave my people out of this shit. My mother should have been payment enough."

Rayjon pointed at a White Castle burger joint. "Bruh, put that bitch-nigga on the floor back there while I order this food. I'm hungry as a muthafucka." He said this before parking and jumping out of the car.

I knew right then this nigga was out of his mind. Who the fuck stopped at a restaurant to get some-thing to eat while they were on a mission? That shit blew my mind and made me even more sick because I knew he wasn't playin' wit' a full deck.

Ten minutes later he came back wit' four bags of food and passed three of them out to his goons. These fuck-niggaz actually had the audacity to eat they shit while taking turns holding pistols to my head until they finished their meals.

Rayjon started up the truck and pulled out of the parking lot, burping in the process. "Racine, wasn't no way I was finna be able to chop yo' daughter and yo' bitch up on an empty stomach. Yo' momma wore me out. That bitch was turning this way and that. Then all that blood was just ridiculous. I know yo' daughter got her genes, so I'ma have to kill her in the bathtub. That way her blood can go right down the drain," he said before using a toothpick to get at the meat in his teeth.

Hearing him talk about my child like she was nothin' was killing my soul. It made me feel so weak and broken. Here this nigga was talking about killing my baby, and I couldn't do shit about it. It was a feeling I couldn't even put into words.

"Aw, yeah, far as me killing you and letting them go?" He shook his head. "That shit ain't happening. That'd put a black eye in the game, and I can't do that. I live for this shit, and I'ma die by the code of the slums. My mother and father died living this life, so it's meant for me to carry on their legacy. This shit is bred deep within me, and you gon' learn that real fast. Oh, and don't think yo' cousin getting off the hook, either, 'cause when we find that fuck-nigga, he gon' spend a few nights with the maggots, word is bond."

When we pulled up in front of my house, I felt like throwing up, especially when Rayjon got out of the truck with his pistol in his hand. It had to be about four in the morning. It was still dark outside. I watched him walk up the steps and ring the doorbell. I sat there shaking like a leaf, praying Kenosha had taken my daughter anywhere. I just prayed God would let me skate on this one, but all my hope shattered when I saw the porch light come on and the curtain move away from the window.

178

I knew I fucked up right away because Kenosha had seen Rayjon wit' me on numerous occasions, and I never got around to telling her I was beefing wit' the nigga now, so she should stay clear of him.

When she opened the door and he forced his way in, I heard her scream, and then I felt blood pouring out of my nose. I was worrying that bad. Minutes later, he came back out of the house and motioned for us to come in.

As soon as I got through the threshold, I saw he had Kenosha laying on her stomach in the living room, right next to my daughter. His goons slung me to the floor right beside them.

Kenosha screamed when she saw me. "Racine, baby, what's going on? Why is Rayjon doing this to us?" she whimpered.

Rayjon laughed. "Yeah, Racine. Why don't you tell yo' bitch how you played me out my cash and used my bitch to do it. Tell this ho' why I gotta kill her and yo' daughter before I whack you right behind them because you double-crossed me on some fuck-nigga shit."

Kenosha tried to get up. "Kill?"

Rayjon flung her back down and sat on her back, putting his gun to the back of her head while Madison cried beside her. "Bitch, if you try that shit one mo' time, I'ma knock yo' head off yo' shoulders. Now, stay yo' punk-ass down!" He put his forearm into the back of her neck roughly.

I tried to get up, but they still had my hands and ankles tied together, making it hard. Not only that, but one of his goons had a shotgun to the back of my head. "Kenosha, just stay down, baby. We gon' figure all of this shit out, I promise."

Rayjon put more of his weight onto her. "That's definitely a promise he just broke to you, bitch, because all three of you muthafuckas finna die. You can bet yo' bottom dolla' on that shit."

Kenosha exhaled loudly and sounded like she was having a hard time breathing. "Rayjon, please, get off me. I'm pregnant, and you're hurting me. I can barely breathe," she said, sounding winded.

"Daddy, I'm scared. I don't wanna be out here wit' y'all. I'm scared of these men," Madison whimpered and rolled closer to me.

One of Rayjon's goons snatched her up by her hair and held her in the air while she screamed at the top of her lungs.

"Come on, man. Let my daughter go, Rayjon. This shit ain't cool, nigga. This shit between me and you. Now, I done told you that you can get all yo' money back, along wit' yo' dope, then you can kill me. Just let my people go," I said, feeling my heart beat faster and faster.

In response to me, Rayjon yanked up Kenosha while his goon placed his hand around Madison's mouth and his other goon picked me up and kept his shotgun pointed at the back of my head. We traveled through the house until we wound up downstairs in the basement, sitting on the concrete with our backs against the wall. Kenosha and I had shotguns pointed at our foreheads while Madison snuggled her head into my underarm, crying and begging for me to protect her. "I'm so scared, daddy. I'm so, so scared," she sobbed. I could feel her body shaking, and it broke my heart.

Rayjon stopped pacing and clapped his hands together one time, really loud. "Fuck, I got it. I know what I'ma do." He walked over to me with an evil grin on his face before squatting down in front of me. "You know what I'ma do for you? I'm gon' throw you a bone since I did kill yo' mother and shit. This what I'ma do. Nigga, you gon' pay me three million dollars in cash before May first. You also gon' bring me Averie's head in a bag, along wit' yo' cousin's. And in exchange for all of that, I'm gon' let one of them live, and I'm gon' let you pick which one you gon' kill. It's gon' come down to who you love the most. Is it gon' be yo' daughter, or yo' pregnant-ass baby mother? I'ma giving you five minutes to figure shit out and take this deal."

Submission Guideline.

Submit the first three chapters of your completed manuscript to ldpsubmissions@gmail.com, subject line: Your book's title. The manuscript must be in a .doc file and sent as an attachment. Document should be in Times New Roman, double spaced and in size 12 font. Also, provide your synopsis and full contact information. If sending multiple submissions, they must each be in a separate email.

Have a story but no way to send it electronically? You can still submit to LDP/Ca$h Presents. Send in the first three chapters, written or typed, of your completed manuscript to:

LDP: Submissions Dept
Po Box 870494
Mesquite, Tx 75187

DO NOT send original manuscript. Must be a duplicate.

Provide your synopsis and a cover letter containing your full contact information.

Thanks for considering LDP and Ca$h Presents.

Coming Soon from Lock Down Publications/Ca$h Presents

BOW DOWN TO MY GANGSTA

By **Ca$h**

TORN BETWEEN TWO

By **Coffee**

BLOOD STAINS OF A SHOTTA **III**

By **Jamaica**

WHEN THE STREETS CLAP BACK **III**

By **Jibril Williams**

STEADY MOBBIN

By **Marcellus Allen**

BLOOD OF A BOSS **V**

By **Askari**

LOYAL TO THE GAME **IV**

By **T.J. & Jelissa**

A DOPEBOY'S PRAYER **II**

By **Eddie "Wolf" Lee**

IF LOVING YOU IS WRONG... **III**

LOVE ME EVEN WHEN IT HURTS

By **Jelissa**

DAUGHTERS OF A SAVAGE **II**

By **Chris Green**

SKI MASK CARTEL **III**

By **T.J. Edwards**

TRAPHOUSE KING **II**

By **Hood Rich**

BLAST FOR ME **II**

RAISED AS A GOON **V**

By **Ghost**

ADDICTIED TO THE DRAMA **III**

By **Jamila Mathis**

LIPSTICK KILLAH **II**

By **Mimi**

WHAT BAD BITCHES DO **2**

By **Aryanna**

THE COST OF LOYALTY **II**

By **Kweli**

SHE FELL IN LOVE WITH A REAL ONE

By **Tamara Butler**

LOVE SHOULDN'T HURT

By **Meesha**

Available Now

RESTRAINING ORDER **I & II**

By **CA$H & Coffee**

LOVE KNOWS NO BOUNDARIES **I II & III**

By **Coffee**

RAISED AS A GOON I, II, III & IV

BRED BY THE SLUMS I, II, III

BLAST FOR ME

By **Ghost**

LAY IT DOWN **I & II**

LAST OF A DYING BREED

BLOOD STAINS OF A SHOTTA I & II

By **Jamaica**

LOYAL TO THE GAME

LOYAL TO THE GAME II

LOYAL TO THE GAME III

By **TJ & Jelissa**

BLOODY COMMAS I & II

SKI MASK CARTEL I & II

By **T.J. Edwards**

IF LOVING HIM IS WRONG…I & II

By **Jelissa**

WHEN THE STREETS CLAP BACK I & II

By **Jibril Williams**

A DISTINGUISHED THUG STOLE MY HEART I II & III

By **Meesha**

PUSH IT TO THE LIMIT

By **Bre' Hayes**

BLOOD OF A BOSS **I, II, III & IV**

By **Askari**

THE STREETS BLEED MURDER **I, II & III**

THE HEART OF A GANGSTA I II& III

By **Jerry Jackson**

CUM FOR ME

CUM FOR ME 2

CUM FOR ME 3

An **LDP Erotica Collaboration**

BRIDE OF A HUSTLA **I & II**

THE FETTI GIRLS **I, II& III**

By **Destiny Skai**

WHEN A GOOD GIRL GOES BAD

By **Adrienne**

A GANGSTER'S REVENGE **I II III & IV**

THE BOSS MAN'S DAUGHTERS

THE BOSS MAN'S DAUGHTERS II

THE BOSSMAN'S DAUGHTERS III

THE BOSSMAN'S DAUGHTERS IV

A SAVAGE LOVE **I & II**

BAE BELONGS TO ME

A HUSTLER'S DECEIT I, II

By **Aryanna**

A KINGPIN'S AMBITON

A KINGPIN'S AMBITION **II**

I MURDER FOR THE DOUGH

By **Ambitious**

TRUE SAVAGE

TRUE SAVAGE II

TRUE SAVAGE **III**

DAUGHTERS OF A SAVAGE

By **Chris Green**

A DOPEBOY'S PRAYER

By **Eddie "Wolf" Lee**

THE KING CARTEL **I, II & III**

By **Frank Gresham**

THESE NIGGAS AIN'T LOYAL **I, II & III**

By **Nikki Tee**

GANGSTA SHYT **I II &III**

By **CATO**

THE ULTIMATE BETRAYAL

By **Phoenix**

BOSS'N UP **I , II & III**

By **Royal Nicole**

I LOVE YOU TO DEATH

By Destiny J

I RIDE FOR MY HITTA

I STILL RIDE FOR MY HITTA

By **Misty Holt**

LOVE & CHASIN' PAPER

By **Qay Crockett**

TO DIE IN VAIN

By **ASAD**

BROOKLYN HUSTLAZ

By **Boogsy Morina**

BROOKLYN ON LOCK I & II

By **Sonovia**

GANGSTA CITY

By **Teddy Duke**

A DRUG KING AND HIS DIAMOND I & II

A DOPEMAN'S RICHES

By Nicole Goosby

TRAPHOUSE KING

By **Hood Rich**

T.J. Edwards

BOOKS BY LDP'S CEO, CA$H

TRUST IN NO MAN

TRUST IN NO MAN 2

TRUST IN NO MAN 3

BONDED BY BLOOD

SHORTY GOT A THUG

THUGS CRY

THUGS CRY 2

THUGS CRY 3

TRUST NO BITCH

TRUST NO BITCH 2

TRUST NO BITCH 3

TIL MY CASKET DROPS

RESTRAINING ORDER

RESTRAINING ORDER 2

IN LOVE WITH A CONVICT

Coming Soon

BONDED BY BLOOD 2

BOW DOWN TO MY GANGSTA

Made in the USA
Middletown, DE
21 July 2019